Second Thoughts about the Heir

Second Time Brides, Book 3

By
Sky Purington

ARE YOU SIGNED UP FOR DRAGONBLADE'S BLOG?

You'll get the latest news and information on exclusive giveaways, exclusive excerpts, coming releases, sales, free books, cover reveals and more.

Check out our complete list of authors, too!

No spam, no junk. That's a promise!

Sign Up Here

www.dragonbladepublishing.com

Dearest Reader;

Thank you for your support of a small press. At Dragonblade Publishing, we strive to bring you the highest quality Historical Romance from some of the best authors in the business. Without your support, there is no 'us', so we sincerely hope you adore these stories and find some new favorite authors along the way.

Happy Reading!

CEO, Dragonblade Publishing

Additional Dragonblade Books by Author Sky Purington

Second Time Brides Series
Never Second Guess a Lord (Book 1)
The Secondhand Earl (Book 2)
Second Thoughts about the Heir (Book 3)
Harrowing Hall (Novella)

Highlander's Pact Series
Scoundrel's Vengeance (Book 1)
Scoundrel's Fortune (Book 2)
Scoundrel's Redemption (Book 3)

The Lyon's Den Series
To Tame the Lyon

Pirates of Britannia Series
The Seafaring Rogue
The Sea Hellion

Blackmail turns to scandalous desire in this enemies-to-lovers romance.

Done mourning a husband who was three times her age, Lady Abigail Somerset is ready for adventure. She begins by pretending to be a commoner at a tavern. More daring still, when she bumps into a handsome American who appears equally as common, she gives him the impression that she is a lady of the night. Naturally, the moment she learns he is en route to the same Scottish castle as she, she sets the record straight and makes a hasty departure.

Determined to open unattainable doors to his businesses, Laurence Wright, heir to the Wright fortune, is determined to marry into the English peerage. Little does he know the beautiful commoner he runs into at a bar ends up being an aristocrat in disguise. As ruthless in love as he is in business, he decides he will make Abigail his, no matter what. Even if it means threatening to share her naughty tavern persona and ruining her good name. More than that, he'll succeed even if making her his wife endangers the heart he'd had no idea existed.

Chapter One

Somerset, England
8 November 1818

L
ADY ABIGAIL, OR Abby to those who knew her best, stepped out the front door of her late husband's townhome for the last time and breathed in the fresh autumn air with relief. She was out of mourning and finally free. Without a man to answer to until her dying breath if she had her way. Eager for what lay ahead, she did not look back but instead climbed into the waiting coach and sat beside her lady's maid, Eleanor.

"This is very exciting, is it not, my lady?" Eleanor's sage-green eyes twinkled with anticipation. "A true adventure, to be sure."

She'd hired Eleanor after dismissing the stern-faced lady's maid her deceased husband had originally hired for her. While not a great beauty, she was pretty and kind-hearted. Better still, she was a bubbly sort who saw the world through the lens of youth and hope. Both had been taken from Abby when Reginald decided to make her his wife soon after her coming-out ball, so she found Eleanor's demeanor refreshing.

"This is very exciting indeed." She met Eleanor's smile and squeezed her hand. "Just wait until you see MacLauchlin Castle. You shall love it straight away, my dear."

Even though Abby had been left well off by a stipend from

Reginald's estate, she'd decided to put off purchasing a new home and stay with her sister Maude and brother-by-marriage, Blake. Take the time to visit friends and decide where she would like to live rather than be confined to any one location immediately.

So, starting her new life at MacLauchlin Castle seemed the perfect location to spread her wings. Her sister loved entertaining, so interesting people were always coming and going, meaning there were new friends to be made. Truly, the friendships she'd made thus far had kept her afloat during her marriage to Reginald. Sadly, she'd seen less and less of them during the last few years of his life, when he'd grown so dependent on her.

"Good morning, dear friends." Abby smiled at her friend, Margaret, and her husband, Robert, when they stopped soon after to pick them up. They were all en route to the same place, so they'd decided to travel together. She was thankful for it, too, as traveling so far without male companionship or some sort of escort was unwise.

Margaret and Robert were a pair well-matched with kindred personalities, pleasing dispositions, and complementary figures. Where Margaret was rather curvy, Robert was quite slender.

"Good morning." Margaret's dark brown eyes were especially merry when she met Abby's smile. "How *excited* you must be, darling."

"More than you can imagine."

She had met Margaret and her sister Isabella when they were girls and had remained fast friends since. While she saw Margaret more often, as they lived close, she had not seen Isabella in some time. Like her, Isabella was recently widowed, so they looked forward to seeing one another at Maude and Blake's Martinmas celebration.

While she would have liked to ride straight to MacLauchlin Castle, the commute was too long, so they would spend the night at an inn along the way, which presented the trio with an opportunity that could be great fun. So at her request, and always up for a bit of fun as well, her friends had dressed plainly to avoid unwanted attention.

Rather, seeing the bit of adventure in it, they had dressed to blend in.

What game did they have in mind? They would not be aristocrats at the inn because she longed to be free of it all for just one night. Free of the endless expectations she had suffered her entire life. Instead, she wanted to be a normal woman for a few short hours.

Forever grateful for their light-hearted manners, she noted their traveling clothes. "I do appreciate your playing along."

"But of course." Margaret grinned at Robert. "We do so love an adventure from time to time, do we not, my dear?"

"Indeed." Robert smiled from Margaret to Abby before he grew rather serious. "Yet, I must remind you to be careful and not wander too far from our sides."

She did her best to look most serious. "You have my word."

Having looked forward to this evening for some time, she had chosen her clothing carefully, opting for a green linen dress that complemented her eyes and crimson curls quite well. Granted, it was a tad daring, accentuating her waistline, and bust rather nicely, but she could not help herself. Was she not allowed to be a bit bold after wearing such drab mourning clothes for a year?

As it turned out, the inn and attached tavern were wonderfully busy and full of a delightful cornucopia of people when she returned downstairs after freshening up in her room. The air smelled of ale, baked bread, and rather strong perfumes. Because they were traveling incognito, they were treated like any other, and she spied her friends standing on the other side of the busy room, waiting for a table.

Determined to enjoy herself, she returned men's smiles as she squeezed her way along, becoming so distracted by the variety of people in the crush, she walked straight into a broad chest. At least, it felt that way due to his substantial height.

The hum of the busy room faded into the background when

his hands came around her upper arms as if to steady her, and her gaze drifted up to his remarkably handsome face. His thick, tousled locks were a sun-streaked dark blond, and his unfashionably tan, chiseled features were difficult to look away from. His deep-set dark blue eyes caught her attention the most, though. They had an unusual way of pulling one in and demanding one's attention.

"My apologies." His deep voice curled through her in a most unexpected way, regardless of his rather hard-sounding accent. "I seem to have run straight into you."

"You are American," she exclaimed, dismayed to find her voice more of a hoarse whisper. Probably a good thing, as she almost spoke with her highborn accent rather than a cockney-sounding one. So, she tried again, sure to sound less herself. "You are American."

And such a splendid way to begin her adventure, as an American would only ever be a pleasant dalliance. Even in the right circles, it could never be anything more. And in this case, he would be a man she would never see again after today.

"I *am* American." He issued a dimple-revealing smile that made him that much more glorious. "And you are English, perhaps?"

"Of course." What else would she be? "Is our accent so foreign to you then, good sir?"

"The name is Laurence." Amusement crinkled the corners of his eyes as he let her arms go more slowly than he might have. "And I only asked because you sound a bit Scottish."

Good Lord, was her accent *that* off? She had thought it rather convincing. Thinking quickly, she came up with a plausible explanation.

"I spent some time in Scotland growing up, so perhaps that is what you hear." Overly aware of his proximity in the thickening crowd, not to mention the unnerving way his gaze lingered on her face, she met his smile. "Nice to meet you, Laurence. My name is Abby."

"A beautiful name." He waved over the barkeep. "May I buy you a drink, Abby?"

"I would like that." Quite a bit, actually, and to be daring indeed as proper ladies did not drink such. "Ale, if you will."

"An ale, it is." His gaze remained on her as he ordered two ales and absently set a coin on the bar top. "So, what brings you here on such a busy night? Do you live in town?"

"No, just passing through," she said. "I am traveling to visit a friend farther north."

"As am I." His smile only broadened. "So we best enjoy ourselves in what short window we have together."

"Perhaps we should." A thrill of anticipation rushed through her, and she batted her lashes at him. "Within reason, of course."

"Of course." He leaned a little closer and quirked the corner of his mouth. "Though I admit to being curious about what you consider *reasonable*."

"This, naturally," she teased, just imagining the possibilities. What would it feel like to throw caution to the wind and kiss a perfect stranger? More pointedly, finally kiss a man closer to her age? "Whatever did you think I meant?"

"It sounded rather open to interpretation." His voice deepened even more, and desire flared in his eyes when his gaze dropped to her lips. "And I admit, I would not be opposed. Not in the least. Just tell me your going rate, and I will pay it."

Her going *what*? That's when it occurred to her what this was. *Whom* he thought she was. While she should slap him for his assumption, she supposed she *had* acted rather forward.

"In fact, I will double it." He traced her jawline with his warm fingers, sending shivers of awareness through her. "Triple it if you say 'yes.'"

She should pull away and set things straight, but she could not seem to do it when she'd become far too aware of him. Aware of how very close he stood and the heat of his strong body. The room faded away altogether until it seemed they stood alone with nothing but the sound of her thudding heart. For a moment, she allowed herself to imagine what it would feel like to accept his proposal.

To become a woman of the night and take him between her thighs.

To make love to someone who looked like him, rather than a husband over three times her age. She had heard there was pleasure to be found in the arms of certain men but had never felt it. Lovemaking with Reginald had been, for the most part, non-existent.

"You could not afford me," she murmured before she could stop herself. Although shocked she had uttered such, she could not help but thrill at just how outside her townhome she had stepped now. Dauntingly far, at that.

"Are you certain?" He ran the pad of his thumb over her lower lip as though measuring how it might feel against his mouth. "Because I find myself willing to spend a great deal indeed to taste you." His gaze swept over her body before returning to her face. "Every last bit of you."

Quick to imagine it, she felt afire and struggled to catch her breath. Reginald had certainly never done anything like that. He would have found it most inappropriate, which was fortunate. At least when it came to him. However, picturing this rogue American doing *those* things seemed quite believable, given the blatant lust in his eyes.

More so, she suspected he would make sure she enjoyed it.

"Ah, there you are, Laurence." An ebony-haired Irishman, nearly as tall and handsome as Laurence, joined them. Admiration lit his pale-green eyes when he looked at her. "And not alone, I see."

"Most certainly not." Laurence handed her one of two ales that had been delivered and waved over another as he introduced them. "Joseph is an old friend, Abby."

"An old friend despite the ocean between you?" She sipped her bitter ale and tried not to flinch. "How did you two meet?"

"We met in Boston years ago." Joseph thanked the barkeep

when he delivered a third ale in record time. "Our families were in business together."

"So that is where you are from?" she asked Laurence. "Boston?"

"It is." He perked an eyebrow. "Ever been?"

"I am afraid not." *If only.* "I have never been outside England."

"Besides Scotland," he reminded her, his gaze curious. "Where you developed a bit of an accent."

Blast it. She had best get her stories straight. "Oh, yes, Scotland, too."

"What part of Scotland?" Joseph wondered.

"A little way over the border." She waved it off. "A small town. Nowhere special."

"Ah." Joseph eyed her a little too knowingly and tapped his lips in contemplation with the pad of his forefinger. "I dare say you possess an unusual accent, even for an Englishwoman who spent time in Scotland."

She imagined she did. Fortunately, he did not go on about it.

"It just so happens we are traveling north of the border," Joseph commented.

"Is that right?"

"Indeed," Laurence said. "To MacLauchlin Castle. Perhaps you have heard of it?"

It felt like the ground dropped out from beneath her. *Truly?* Of all the damnable luck.

Even though Laurence had seemed determined to pay a great deal for her *services*, he and Joseph did not seem richly dressed, so perhaps they were extra staff for the upcoming festivities. Either way, she'd already dug herself a deep enough hole. Most especially if they saw her at the castle and spread rumors below stairs about what had transpired between her and Laurence. She might be up for a grand adventure but still had her good name to consider.

"It has been a pleasure meeting you both." She waved at

Margaret as though her friend had called her over. "But I am afraid my friends await me."

Laurence glanced her friends' way in confusion, then caught her hand when she tried to sidle past him. "Will I see you later?" His voice dropped an octave. A mix of concern and desire flared in his eyes. "Tell me I will see you, Abby. That you will accept my offer."

"I am afraid you misunderstood, good sir." She pulled her hand free. "I am not what you think I am. That said, I beg you to leave me be as I need to get back to my friends."

She prayed he did not follow as she made her way to Margaret and Robert, who seemed amused upon her arrival.

"You seem quite popular, dear friend," Margaret remarked. "Even without your finery, you draw many an eye."

"As long as it is not theirs." She kept her back to Laurence and Joseph. "Tell me the two men I was just chatting with have lost interest in me."

"I cannot speak for the darker-haired one, but the other most certainly has not," Margaret said, amused. "Can you not feel his gaze boring through your back? It seems you rather should, as it has not strayed from you since you left his side."

"Because he is under a false impression," she muttered under her breath.

Margaret's eyebrows swept up. "Whatever do you mean?"

"I mean that I may have led him to believe I was…" *How to phrase it?* "Far more available than I am." When Margaret eyed her in continued confusion, she went on. "I fear for the fun of it, of course, that I might have given him the impression I was…*working*, so to speak."

"Bloody hell, surely *not?*" Robert exclaimed, understanding.

"Oh, I think she very much did." Margaret's eyes rounded, and she chuckled. "You did end up setting him straight, did you not, love?" Her gaze was not nearly as discreet as she thought when she glanced from Laurence to Abby. "Based on how he leans back against the bar now and continues eyeing you, it seems perhaps not."

"I most certainly *did*." She nodded once and prayed he lost interest. "If he still stares, it is because Americans do not know any better." Before they could reply, she flinched and looked at them most seriously. "Yet I fear my tale grows more unfortunate still."

"More unfortunate than giving a strange man, no less an American, the impression you were available at a price?" Robert looked skyward and shook his head. "Dare I ask?"

"No need, darling, as it is clear she is bracing to tell us," Margaret pointed out, smirking. "And she does seem braced to deliver monumental news indeed."

Abby scrunched her nose and gave them the worst of it. "They are traveling to MacLauchlin Castle, too."

This time Margaret bypassed a mere chuckle, tossed her head back, and released a peal of laughter. "Oh, dear heavens, how *grand* your first adventure is, to be sure!" She glanced from the men to Abby again. "Surely, they work below stairs, yes? Not that it makes much difference what class one is when it comes to such scandalous gossip."

"The darker-haired one does look quite familiar," Robert said absently. His brow furrowed. "Perhaps he served me upon my last visit there?"

Whether he did or not, neither of the men approached Abby for the remainder of the evening, and when next she glanced their way, there was no sign of them. Nor did they cross paths again the next morning despite a small, very naughty part of her hoping they might.

"So, what will you do if you see them at MacLauchlin Castle?" Margaret wondered as their coach made its way north. Amusement lit her eyes. "Because I would think it rather awkward if you remain silent when one of them serves you a drink or an hors d'oeuvre."

"Yet we remain silent all the time when staff serves us." Lord, she hoped that did not happen. "So, it would be most acceptable."

"One would think." Margaret found as much humor in Abby's predicament today as she had yesterday. "Yet I highly suspect the taller one will not remain silent. Not with the way he stared at you all night." She shook her head. "He was not shy about it, either, which tells me he would not be shy about speaking plainly with you no matter how much it might jeopardize his employment."

"While employing an Irishman would be something the MacLauchlins would do, I dare say it odd to hire an American." Robert gave them a look. "Especially given Maude's brother-by-marriage, Charles. I would think it unpleasant for him to be around such."

A former navy captain during wartime, her sister Grace's husband had lost an eye and been scarred battling the Americans, so Robert might be right.

"Well, whomever Blake and Maude may or may not hire, Laurence, I mean the taller one, said he was going to MacLauchlin Castle, and he was not dressed richly." She shook her head. "Not at all."

"Nor were you," Margaret reminded. "Yet you are no servant." She shrugged. "So perhaps the two of them were playing the same game as we."

"I certainly hope not." Because them being guests of the MacLauchlins would be even worse.

Suffice it to say, Abby did her best to put it from her mind and felt rather confident that by the time their coach arrived at MacLauchlin Castle, all would be well. How could she not when Maude, in typical Maude fashion, flew down the front stairs and flung her arms around her the moment she stepped out of the coach?

"Dear, lovely sister, I have so looked forward to your arrival." Maude held her at arm's length and looked her over. "How are you feeling? I know you claimed yourself much improved in your letters, but one never necessarily knows the truth of things via such correspondence, do they?"

"I am very well." She smiled and took in the old-world castle with its towers and battlements. "And I am very much looking forward to my stay here. What fun we shall have."

"Indeed, we will. So *very* much fun." Maude greeted Margaret and Robert, then linked arms with Abby and begged them to follow her up the stairs. "Preparations for the Feast of St. Martin are well underway, and guests are already arriving."

"How lovely."

"Yes, truly very lovely." Excitement flashed in Maude's eyes as her butler Finlay held the front door open. "In fact, two esteemed guests arrived just before you, and you will *never* believe who they are."

Forget the floor vanishing from beneath her. She would have much preferred to disappear altogether when said guests turned her way upon entering.

Maude gestured at Joseph first, who was dressed smartly. "Lady Abigail, I give you the Duke of Leinster." She looked Laurence's way, who was just as well dressed now. "And our dear friend Laurence Wright, heir to the infamous Wright fortune."

Chapter Two

THE MOMENT LAURENCE spied Abby coming down the stairs at the tavern, he wanted her. Not to marry, of course, but most certainly to lie with. Had he ever seen a more ravishing woman? Likely not, and he had seen his fair share. She was a cut above the rest with her silky auburn hair, big, thickly lashed, emerald-green eyes, and a light dusting of barely-there freckles kissing her cheekbones that one could only see if they stood very close.

If her delicate features were not stunning enough, her luscious figure certainly was. She was built for a man's arms, from her full breasts to her tiny waist to the flare of her hips. More specifically, she was built for his arms, and he fully intended to enjoy her before everything was said and done. A goal that was only driven home when he made sure they bumped into one another, and he touched her. When he drew in her sweet, flowery scent and felt the undeniable attraction between them.

How pleased he had been to discover she came at a price, then equally dismayed when she said she did not. Such hadn't kept her from his thoughts, however. Rather, she was all he could think about for the remainder of the night. Granted, they had exchanged very few words, but it did not matter. He intended for them to share more. At least enough to get her into his bed.

Yet he had honored her wishes, stayed away, and most certainly regretted it.

"You best put her from your mind, friend," Joseph counseled as they made their way north the next day. "Even if you could find her again, she's not what you are looking for. Best you remember that if you hope to marry into the British ton."

"Why, when they are notorious for keeping mistresses?" He knew nothing of love, so he certainly was not in it for that. Nor did he imagine, given his considerable wealth, an Englishwoman would be looking for a love match either. Not when she could enjoy his money and the esteem that came with it.

"Aristocratic Englishmen might be notorious for mistresses, but you are not English, nor of their caliber, in their opinion." Joseph shook his head. "Rather, I suspect you will need to be on your best behavior if you hope to secure an English wife."

Nothing sounded more boring, but he knew his friend was right. Best he play by their stuffy rules if he meant to accomplish his goals. Once his wife was secured, a great many doors that had been shut to him and his business ventures would open.

So, he did his best to put the vivacious redhead from his mind. No easy task, given her effect on him, from how excited he had grown when he thought he might soon be between her thighs to how intrigued he'd become when she turned him away. Women did not typically turn from him, but she had, and quickly at that, despite being as attracted to him as he was to her. Or so he assumed their attraction was mutual, based on her response to him at the tavern.

Their draw to one another had been unquestionable. Impossible to ignore.

"I am surprised you thought her available for coin," Joseph had said afterward, amused. "Her fair skin is far too soft, and her hair too well groomed for her to be a trollop in these parts. They are a much harder sort and certainly not allowed in establishments like this." He had narrowed his eyes in Abby's direction. "No, I suspect, based on that awful attempt at a rougher accent, that she and her friends play at the same game as we."

"You think her an aristocrat?" *Might he be so lucky.* "English, or Scottish?"

"Hard to know." Joseph had considered her companions. "Though I dare say her friends are very much English. They might try to hide it, but the English peerages tend to have a stiff upper lip we Irish learned to spot centuries ago."

"Indeed." And he was not looking forward to it in an Englishwoman. He had heard they were notoriously put off by intimacy and were horrible gossips besides, so he fully understood their husbands keeping mistresses. "Then, given her daring ways, I can only imagine Abby is Scottish."

This was unfortunate because she seemed the opposite of everything he had heard about ladies of the ton. A non-conformist for certain. Especially considering how well she had flirted. How forward and quite deceitful she'd been, playing on his desire.

"It would make sense she was Scottish, given her abrupt departure when we mentioned MacLauchlin Castle." Joseph continued contemplating her. "Which, I must say, thickens the plot. Might we see her again amongst the upper crust?" A small smile had hovered on his face when he'd looked at Laurence. "That would be something given what she just led you to believe, would it not?"

"It would." And great fun if he were pursuing a Scotswoman, but, alas, he was not. "Yet doubtful on all counts."

Doubtful, that is, until he arrived at MacLauchlin Castle.

Better still, when none other than Abby, better known as Lady Abigail Somerset, walked into the great hall in all her finery with a very aristocratic British accent. If that were not fortunate enough, against all odds, she was Maude's widowed sister. Ironically, she was the very woman Blake had written him and Joseph about, so she was very much available.

Unbelievably, neither he nor Joseph had put two and two together but then what were the chances a proper Englishwoman would pull such a stunt? Granted, Blake had referred to her as a daring sort, but honestly, he imagined that meant she was only a tad less dull and stiff than her female counterparts. He could never have anticipated this, *her*, because his friend seemed very much right.

Wonderfully right, in this case.

He could tell Joseph bit back his surprise and no doubt amusement as they bid her hello. Where Joseph offered a brief bow from the waist, Laurence took it one step further, bowed, lifted her gloved hand, and ever-so-gently pressed his lips to the back of it.

"It is a pleasure to meet you, Lady Somerset." He allowed his lips to linger and, much like the night before, eyed her with unabashed appreciation. While he would have preferred to feel her soft flesh against his lips, he enjoyed the startled look in her eyes and the increasing rosiness of her dainty cheeks. "I trust your journey here was pleasant?"

"It was, thank you." She pulled her hand away and seemed to gather herself when she looked Maude's way. "I find I am most weary and in need of rest, sister."

"Of course." Maude looked at Abby with concern. "You do look quite flushed all of a sudden. Are you well?"

"I will be once I rest." She bid Joseph and Laurence a good day with a rather stiff nod to each of them. "Your Grace. Mr. Wright."

Rather than overly engage them, the couple with whom she had traveled, an earl and his wife no less, bid them a pleasant afternoon and made themselves scarce as well. Meanwhile, he watched Abby until she vanished upstairs with her sister, then grinned at Joseph. "It seems I am lucky indeed because I have finally met my future wife."

"No doubt you think you have, but she will not be a prize so easily won, if at all," he reminded. "As you well know from Blake, she has no desire to remarry, nor does she need your money."

"Even so." He shrugged. "She is in need of an adventure or two, yes? Were those not MacLauchlin's very words? And he would know, given he and Maude are becoming quite notorious for their matchmaking skills." He winked. "So, I will give her that adventure. Several adventures, for that matter."

"Without doubt, you will try, but I fear you are only headed for heartache, my friend," Joseph warned. "Blake claims her marriage to the late Viscount of Somerset was quite unfortunate. He was old enough to be her grandfather and quite stodgy. If that were not bad enough, he was too embarrassed to hire a professional after he ended up in a gouty chair and made Abigail see to his needs." He winced and shook his head. "I cannot imagine a woman wanting to be anywhere near another marriage after that."

Nor could he, yet he would have her if it were the last thing he did. He'd succeeded at everything he set his mind to, and this would be no different. And now the pot had grown even sweeter because he would enjoy not just her title but her lush little body. When that happened, he would taste everything that had been so swiftly denied him the night before. She obviously wanted love no more than he, so it would be the perfect arrangement.

A marriage of convenience that would satisfy them both a great deal.

"Ah, there you are, old chaps," Blake declared, smiling as he joined them. He clasped Joseph's shoulder and shook Laurence's hand. "I cannot tell you how happy I am to see you again, my friends. It has been far too long." He glanced around. "Apologies I could not greet you sooner. Have you met my wife, Maude, yet?"

"We did." Joseph met Blake's smile. "And she is every bit as lovely as you described her."

"Yes, she is." He urged them to follow him. "Come. Let us share a wee dram before things become too busy."

Never one to turn down good Scottish whisky, he joined his friends in Blake's study. "I recall your castle being impressive, MacLauchlin, but somehow it seems even more so now."

"You can thank my Maude for that." Blake handed them glasses of whisky and urged them to join him on plush leather chairs in front of the fire. "She has breathed new life into this castle and most certainly into me."

MacLauchlin had always struck him as a content sort and an astute businessman, but he could admit his friend seemed nicely rounded off now.

"She is truly enchanting," Laurence praised, meaning it. He had known Maude mere minutes and already liked her. But then, how could he not when she was the opposite of how he had heard English aristocrats were? No surprise, given she was born a commoner. "As is her lovely sister, Lady Abigail."

"Ah, you two have met Abby then?" Blake's expression was difficult to read as he looked from Laurence to Joseph, prompting the Irishman to reply first. "And what did you make of her?"

"I thought her quite interesting." Joseph glanced from Laurence back to Blake, clearly debating how honest he should be. "Undoubtedly a handful, if I were to be honest."

"Indeed, she can be." Blake looked back and forth between them, and his eyebrows pinched. "Might I ask about your first impression of her? Did she seem in such good spirits again, then?"

While MacLauchlin could just as easily be talking about Abby coming out of her mourning period, he got the impression it might have more to do with Joseph calling her a handful.

"She is in pleasant spirits, to be sure," Laurence said before Joseph could answer. He smiled pleasantly at his Irish friend, hoping he understood he intended to keep Abby's secret for now. "She seemed very charming and vivacious, would you not say, Joseph?" He looked at Blake again. "Quite different than many of the other noble ladies I have met. A breath of fresh air." Unable to help himself, he smiled more broadly still. "I would even go so far as to say I would not have thought her an aristocrat upon our first meeting."

"That does sound like our Abby, on occasion." MacLauchlin sipped his whisky and considered the two of them. "You do recall what I said about her in my letters? Maude's goal when it comes to her widowed sisters? To any woman she cares about whom she feels is in need of love?"

"We do." Joseph sipped his whisky as well. "She wants them all happily married off, including Abby, who will never agree to it after her late husband."

"While we rarely disagree on matters like this, I remain convinced Maude fights a losing battle with Abby." Blake sighed. "Even so, at her request and because it has been too long, I invited you, among others, to join in the numerous festivities between now and New Year's Eve. Yet I must warn you once more that I cannot see Abby agreeing to marry either of you, let alone anyone else."

"Understood." Joseph nodded once at Blake in reassurance. "And as we told you, we have business in these parts through the end of the year, anyway, so we merely look at this as an opportunity to reunite with you and get to know your lovely wife better."

Certain he would prove Blake wrong about Abby, Laurence raised his glass in a toast. "Hear, hear, to reunite with old friends."

Both raised their glasses in turn. "Hear, hear."

After that, they spent time catching up and chatting about old times. Not just their days in Scotland and Ireland but in Boston when they were younger. There might be an ocean between them, but they had kept in touch and managed several visits. Even though his blood was "too thinned" for any sort of title, Laurence's family was distantly related to Joseph's, so they considered one another kin. Blake and Joseph also shared a distant bloodline, so one way or another, after meeting and getting along well, the three of them came to consider one another family no matter how different their lots in life.

Eventually, Blake had to see to new arrivals but urged them to enjoy his whisky for as long as they liked.

"We should have been honest with him about Lady Abigail," Joseph said as he refilled their glasses. "He should know what she is capable of for her own safety if nothing else."

"Is she not safe enough above stairs in the cozy confines of her sister's castle?" He wondered if she bathed at this very moment. A means, of course, to wash away the weariness of traveling, or so she would claim. The truth was, he was sure that she had been unsettled by discovering who they were and had run away. "I see no reason to tell Blake and worry him. He knows she is bold, so let that be enough to concern him and his wife for now."

In the meantime, Laurence intended to see to that very boldness. Encourage it, in fact. Watch her break free of the uppity confines her class had crucified her with.

"Even so," Joseph made clear. "If Abby is showing signs of mental instability, Blake should know. *They* should know."

"Good God, man." He rolled his eyes and downed half his whisky. "Abby is anything but unstable. She is but a long-trapped bird finally spreading her wings. Surely, you see that."

"Some *might* see it that way," Joseph conceded. "Where others might see her actions last night too bold by half. So bold she could have ended up ruined if you had been any other lad." He shook his head. "It is one thing to break the chains of confinement. Quite another, to behave so wantonly and put one's good name at risk."

"How very aristocratic you have become, *Your Grace*," he said dryly, finishing off his whisky in one long gulp.

"Is it so aristocratic to care for a woman's well-being?"

"When said with that particular upturn to your chin, I would say so." Yet his friend was not entirely wrong, and he meant to capitalize on it. "To that end, I suggest we closely monitor Abby and keep her around us rather than with those who might mean her harm."

"I highly doubt anyone in MacLauchlin's circles means her harm." Joseph stood and shook his head at Laurence. "But do what you like, friend, as your true intentions are certainly not lost on me. You intend to pursue her at all costs." He stopped at the door on the way out. "I will keep an eye on her, though. Perhaps more than you might like."

At his best when faced with competition, Laurence smiled and held his empty glass up in a mock toast. "Do give it your best shot, old chap."

Rather than pour another, he stared at the fire and wondered how he should go about things.

"Be relentless," his father would have said. "Go after what you want without pause. Without a lick of sentiment, if it means winning yet again. Use whatever it takes to achieve your goals. Utilize whatever weapons are at your disposal, whether cunning or otherwise."

With that in mind, he retired to his chamber, bathed, and dressed in his very finest for dinner and dancing that night. Prepared to go to battle with a stunning lady of the night turned into a member of Society.

"You cut a fine figure, sir," his valet, Harold, praised, straightening his cravat. He was newly hired and British, so Laurence painted just the right picture. "Very well presented, indeed."

"Thank you, Harold." He grinned, happy with his appearance. "You did well, but I fear I need more from you."

Harold might have been on the younger side, but that served Laurence's purpose as the young tended to be more easily molded into what one needed. In this case, a valet who was willing to help him in unorthodox ways.

"Of course, sir." Despite offering a crisp, almost military-like nod, not a single lock of Harold's neatly combed brown hair budged. "Anything you need."

"Information." He pressed several coins into his man's hand. "Anything you can discover about Lady Somerset below stairs. Anything at all."

"Sir, you need not pay me more than you already do, nor should I likely—"

"You should, and you will." He was sure to sound most dire. "For Lady Somerset's well-being, of course, as I intend to ask for her hand eventually. She will become Mrs. Wright soon enough, and I would know everything I can about her beforehand, so I am fully prepared to see to her comfort and needs going forward."

In truth, any information he received was possible fodder for winning her over.

Harold blinked as if caught off guard by that. "But," he stuttered, "are you quite sure, sir?"

"I am." He frowned. "Why ever would I not be?"

"Because she is…" Harold kept rapidly blinking his rather sparse eyelashes as though unsure how to put it. "What I mean to say is…"

"What, man?" He narrowed his eyes. "Spit it out."

"Lady Somerset is the widow of a viscount," Harold finally managed. "And you are…not…a viscount, that is."

Ah, he understood now.

"No, I am not a viscount, earl, duke, or any other member of your precious peerage." Not upset in the least, he winked and grinned. "But I *am* the man Lady Abigail will marry. Mark my words. Until then—" he gestured at the coin in Harold's hand— "find out whatever you can. Even the smallest things matter. Do this, and you will soon be a valet to an aristocrat and looking at a considerable raise." He tilted his head in question. "Does that sound appealing in the least?"

This time Harold did not stutter or blink but saw good sense. "Very much so, sir."

"Excellent." He clasped his valet's shoulder and treated him like a friend rather than an employee. "I look forward to hearing what you discover."

Before Harold could respond, Laurence headed downstairs, eager to lay eyes on Abby again. A tad desperate if he were honest. Uncomfortably desperate if he were even more truthful. There were more people than he expected downstairs, given the holiday was still two days out, but he had never been one to shy away from a crowd. If anything, so many people in one place tended to be his strong suit because there was always a deal to be made or another business venture rife for the taking.

However, the one he was most interested in appeared to be

amiss.

"There you are, Mr. Wright." Maude seemed to appear out of thin air and smiled warmly at him. "Dinner will not be served for a while yet, so I was hoping we might enjoy one another's company?"

"I would like that." He smiled and held out the crook of his elbow. "It has been some time since I last visited. Might we stroll a bit in this beautiful castle of yours?"

"Indeed." She chattered on as though they were old friends. "How did you find your chambers? Do you have everything you need? I dare say Blake would want you most comfortable as he is quite fond of you."

"I am fond of him as well." He nodded. "Yes, my accommodations are well met, my lady. I want for nothing." *Except for being wed to your sister.* "Thank you."

"You need not thank me." Her interest in him was most genuine; Maude's smile never wavered. "My home is your home for as long as you are in these parts." Her eyebrows flew up. "Which I assume will be past the New Year at the very least?"

"You assume correctly." Too curious, he could not help but mention Abby. "I was honored to meet your sister, Lady Somerset, earlier and looked forward to speaking with her again."

"How nice of you, as she could use friends on her road to recovery." Maude surprised him when she grew quite serious. "For she is just out of mourning, you know, and more fragile than she lets on." She sighed sadly and shook her head. "Hence, I am afraid she has decided against joining us this evening."

So she meant to keep hiding, did she?

"I'm sorry to hear that." More than she could imagine. "And surprised to hear she is so fragile." Somehow he found that hard to believe. "If anything, she struck me as rather—" *Flirtatious? Fun? Unforgettable?*—"courageous, if I were to be frank."

"That is a rather astute word considering you only met her briefly upon arrival."

"Astute because of how your husband described her in his

latest letter." He did not play coy because he suspected Maude preferred the opposite. Besides, he rather preferred being forthright when it came to such important matters. "Am I mistaken that you did not know Blake spoke of your sister and the death of her disabled, elderly husband? No doubt spoke of her on your behalf? More to the point, did you not see me and likely others as possible suitors?"

"You are indeed blunt, Mr. Wright."

"Laurence," he insisted. "Please."

"Perhaps eventually." She stopped and considered him. "I admit I long for Abby to find the love she deserves, but I cannot say with certainty that you are a fit for her, Mr. Wright."

"And why is that?"

"Because I cannot figure out how noble your intentions are."

"So, I do not have your support if I pursue her?"

She seemed surprised that he would ask. "Is such necessary?"

"Preferable." He remained candid. "But not necessary."

"I see." She cocked her head. "Why do you think her courageous?"

"Why do you question it?"

"Please," Maude said softly. "Let us not mince words."

While it was on the tip of his tongue to share what Abby had done at the tavern, he decided to stick with what he knew of her through Blake yet put his own spin on the way his friend had phrased things.

"Is it not courageous to marry a man so much older than oneself?" He flinched at the mere thought of it. At the very idea such a great beauty had been wasted on an old pompous fool. "More courageous still, to persevere when he became disabled, and she cared for him herself. I think we can both agree that had to have been an atrocious chore for her, yet she did it regardless, yes?"

"Yes, because she had no choice," Maude said softly, "as most husbands tend to rule all."

He recalled the look in Abby's eyes when their gazes first

connected at the tavern. Sure, there had been flirtation and excitement, but there had also been a raw vulnerability mixed with surprising inner strength. "Perhaps, but I suspect a part of your sister would have cared for Lord Somerset no matter what. That she possesses an inner fortitude, and courage, that most lack."

Maude contemplated him for a moment before she appeared to hear something he did not and offered her apologies. "It seems I am needed elsewhere." She swept away, but not before she stopped at the door she was about to enter and paused, speaking loud enough for him to hear. "You are correct, Mr. Wright. My sister is very courageous. Consistent, too, as every time she and her late husband visited, utilizing a ramp that we have since removed, they stayed in their second-floor chamber on the north-facing side of the castle. If I recall correctly, she particularly enjoyed sitting on its balcony after she saw him to bed."

With that, she was gone, but she had shared more than enough.

Everything he needed to know to begin wooing Lady Abigail quite properly indeed.

Chapter Three

ABBY MIGHT HAVE enjoyed being bold on occasion but wished she could erase her frivolous behavior the evening before the moment she realized who Laurence and Joseph were. How could she have been so utterly foolish?

"How could you have ever known they were a duke of all things and the heir to the Wright fortune?" Margaret said as Eleanor unpinned Abby's hair. Her friend lounged nearby. "How could any of us have known?" Margaret's eyes rounded. "They did not look the part in the least." They rounded even more. "Most certainly not the Duke of Leinster and, goodness knows, not Mr. Wright." She shook her head. "Do you have *any* idea how much he is worth?"

"I couldn't care less." She had heard rumors, and it was enough to easily buy his way into any elite circle. Enough to buy a whole country, for that matter. "They think me a trollop, and that is not something one can come back from."

"Oh, I do not know, my lady." Free to say what she would around Abby, Eleanor grinned. "I think it made you seem rather daring and different than what they must be used to. Memorable, to be sure."

"To be sure, darling," Margaret echoed, sipping her claret. "That said, you should not hide up in this dismal chamber full of memories but join me for the festivities downstairs."

"This chamber is not dismal," she defended it even though it very much was. Everywhere she looked, she saw Reginald needing help with one thing or another those last few years. "It is—" *Horrid? Sad? Better left to the past?*—"mine when I stay here."

"Only because you have not asked for a different room," Eleanor pointed upward. "One as high as you can get to enjoy the view and escape old memories."

"Indeed, love." Margaret raised her glass. "Well said."

Whether it was or not, something inside Abby made it impossible to request; she could not fathom what it was, only that she felt beholden to this chamber and its many memories. Or maybe it was because this room had her "freedom balcony," as she had come to call it years before.

It was a place she was eager to enjoy alone after she had sent Eleanor and Margaret on their way a short time later. Despite the chilly time of year, she shouldered into a warm coat, poured a teeming glass of claret to lose herself in while she ruminated on her tavern disaster, and sat down outside. Why must there always be dour thoughts in this beautiful place? Misery to drown in?

Or at least she tried to ruminate and drown in misery until something bounced off the balcony beside her. A bit off a tree, she imagined, determined to nick her even in her darkest hour. As if the Fates heard her, something landed in her lap.

"You did not come off a tree," she murmured, picking up the small, flat stone.

She no sooner said it than another sailed past her, not from above but from somewhere below. Confused yet curious, she peeked over the edge only to dodge another pebble Laurence threw at her.

"What are you *doing?*" she exclaimed, not so far above him that she need yell. Yet she would certainly raise her voice. "Stop that!"

"I will if you come downstairs and join the festivities, my lady." He shrugged. "Otherwise, it will rain pebbles, and as you saw, my aim is rather good despite the wind."

It *was* gusty out, and her balcony was relatively small, so he had her there.

"Then I will go inside," she declared.

He grabbed the sturdiest-looking vine climbing the castle wall—*her* vine!—and grinned at her. "And I will follow."

How many times had she fantasized about climbing down that vine? Climbing down and escaping the prison her life had become?

"You would not dare climb up," she said, yet highly suspected he would.

"I will, and you know it." He gestured at his fine attire, then looked at her with blatant appreciation. "Put on your loveliest dress, my love, and come spend the evening with your future husband."

"*Husband?*" She laughed. "Surely, you jest."

"Never." He shook his head and then narrowed his eyes in thought. "Well, perhaps on occasion when it suits me, but not when it comes to a woman." He pressed his lips together and flinched. "Well, all right, perhaps when it came to a woman or two, but certainly not you. *Never* you, my little barfly."

She looked right and left, praying nobody was about, and bit back both anger and, irritatingly enough, amusement. "You mock me."

"I do." His smile only grew. "Can you blame me?"

"I can and very much do." She made a gesture that he shove off. "Now I beg you to leave me in peace, kind sir."

"Kind, is it?" He chuckled. "Are we suddenly so formal when just last night—"

"No," she growled when she meant to speak firmly. She wagged her finger back and forth at him. "Whatever you think happened last night did not. It was but a figment of your imagination."

"At least for now." His grin grew more daring, and the way he admired her quite forward. "But it will not be for much longer. Not once you are my wife, and I show you exactly what—"

"Enough." She might occasionally be a tad flirtatious, but he went too far. "Leave now, or I shall scream."

"Then you will not come downstairs?"

"I most certainly will not."

She spun on her heel and started inside, but not before she caught his muttered declaration that he had no choice but to come for her then. While most would call his bluff, she had seen a certain daredevil determination in his eyes last night that told her he was capable of almost anything. So, she returned outside, to find him already halfway up the vine.

"Good God, you *fool*." She held her glass of claret at the ready and narrowed her eyes. "Keep climbing, and I will throw this at you. Do not doubt it for a moment, Mr. Wright."

"Mr. Wright?" He peered up at her and chuckled again. "Given our tavern time and how you led me to believe you were another sort entirely, we should be on a first-name basis at this point, don't you think? Because last night you *were* rather serious there for a moment if I was not mistaken."

"Oh, but you very much were." Despite how right he may be, she was furious at his presumption, so she whipped her glass at him only for it to miss him entirely, shattering onto the ground as it landed.

"I see I must teach you about wind and the objects you choose to fight them with, lovely." He kept climbing. "Did you not notice the pebbles I threw? How flat they were, so they went with the wind, rather than fought it?"

"Go back down," she fumed, trying not to fear for his safety because he deserved no such concern. How to get him down? *Think, Abby.* Something would surely deter him. Perhaps another method of attack? One that tugged on heartstrings she was not sure he possessed? She worked up tears and shook her head. "First, I lost my beloved husband. Now, you mean to take my good name?" She sniffled and wiped away tears that didn't quite exist despite her attempt to create them. "Because if anyone sees you come or go from my chamber, I am ruined. Absolutely *ruined,* and I am *quite* sure I do not deserve that."

"My apologies, my lady." Clearly not buying her tears—not that she blamed him—Laurence kept with that annoying chuckle of his and continued climbing. "I was under the impression last night you cared little for such things."

"Yet I do." She tossed aside the sweets from a plate that had been left for her and held it at the ready to either throw at him or smack him with it if he got too close. Sure to make a show of holding the plate up and narrowing her eyes at its flat dimensions, she nodded with approval. "Now, *this* should work with the wind just fine, so you best make your way back down or else."

Not threatened in the least, he gazed at her with a devilish twinkle in his eyes. "Only if you agree to join me."

"I will not."

Laurence thought about it for a scant little time before he issued a mock-sympathetic expression. "Then perhaps I will have no choice but to share rather unfavorable things about you." He winked. "Not that *I* think they were unfavorable, mind you. I would have rather liked seeing you carry things through last night if you take my meaning."

"You would not *dare* share such and ruin me like that." She planted her free hand on her hip and looked down her nose at him. "And even if you did, I highly doubt people would believe you, considering you are a foreigner and I one of their own."

"Maybe they would, or maybe not." Laurence made a show of thinking it over. "Yet, and tell me if I'm wrong about how your society works, I imagine a great many of your peers would enjoy the gossip whether it was genuine or not." He shrugged, irritatingly matter of fact. "Either way, it matters little if your good name gets ruined because you will be my wife and above them all. Much wealthier, by far." Unbelievably confident, he offered her a crooked grin. "A lady of high society, and I promise you will be far more worshiped in bed than the lot of these upper-crust wives."

Had he *truly* just said that? Lord, he was bold, as well as infuriating. Especially when her traitorous mind wondered just what he meant by that. What he might be capable of in said bed.

"Blast you!" Throwing caution to the wind, she whipped her plate at the damnable American, pleased when it nearly caught him, and he ducked, genuinely threatened.

Or so she thought until he laughed and winked at her again.

"See, it is all about how flat the object is when working with the wind." Nearly close enough to climb over the balcony railing, Laurence nodded once with approval and gestured at her room. "Now go dress and come downstairs so I might woo you properly."

Never so angry but most definitely cornered, she muttered, "Fine," stormed back into her chamber, and slammed the door shut behind her. Unfortunately, giving in to his demands meant ringing the bell for Eleanor to return and help her.

"If I could have managed the ties on this corset alone, I would have," she said as her maid helped her dress a short time later. "I am so sorry if I disturbed you from dinner or whatnot. I had no idea I was dealing with such a loathsome beast."

"You never need be sorry, my lady." Eleanor glanced at Abby's armoire. "Lord Wright is most certainly wrong for doing this. Do you wish to wear something more subdued in hopes of turning his attention elsewhere?"

He had thought her suitable to lay with wearing little more than rags, so even mourning clothes would likely not be good armor.

"Wright is no lord, so do not address him as such." She scowled at her dresses and considered how she wanted to look for the bastard. On second thought, she may have missed him with projectiles, but she could still retaliate against him in a different way.

A thought occurred to her, something provoking. She may have missed him with projectiles; perhaps she could retaliate against him in a different way. "To that end, it should *not* be for him."

"Pardon me, my lady?"

"I believe I shall go about this quite differently." She pointed at her most daring dress. "That one, I think."

She had never worn the lovely emerald-green gown because it had been too low cut in the front for a married woman. Now she was out of mourning and no longer attached, so why not? It was absolutely perfect for what she intended.

"Indeed, my lady?" Eleanor's eyes sparkled with excitement. "Are you quite sure?"

"Very much so."

"Splendid."

And so, she helped Abby into a gown she had long fantasized about finally being able to wear. One that made it very clear she was out of her mourning period and eager to be admired again. What else could it say when she looked in the mirror after Eleanor worked her magic? Her cleavage was notably, almost ridiculously full, and her figure perfectly accentuated.

"You have a way of making me look quite daring, Eleanor," she said softly, gazing at herself in the mirror as her maid draped a shimmering emerald necklace around her neck. She seemed a woman from another lifetime with her hair swept back and long, loose curls framing her face. "A way of making me feel young again."

"That is because you are still quite young, my lady." Eleanor admired her and nodded in co-conspirator approval as she clipped on matching earrings. "And so beautiful, Mr. Wright will never be able to take his eyes off you."

"We can only hope." She stood up straight so that her bosom stood out even more and then shook her head at the shawl Eleanor offered. "Thank you, but no. This battle is best fought with a lack of armor rather than the other way around."

In full agreement, Eleanor opened the door and curtsied. "To a war well fought, my lady."

"Indeed."

The key, of course, was not fighting fair. Or, in this case, fighting until her enemy tired of her antics. That meant beginning her warfare tactics by having Blake called up ahead of time to announce her. Surprise flashed in his eyes when he saw her attire, yet he was ever the gentleman, praising how lovely she looked and that he was glad to see her out of mourning. Then, with a carrying voice, he announced her name and title at the top of the stairs so the many mingling gentlemen below paid attention.

Most especially, Laurence, who, as to be expected, was among them.

"Many thanks, brother." She kissed him on the cheek. "But I must go it alone from here."

Before Blake could deny her and properly escort her down, she started down the stairs, sure to put a little extra sway in her step. Not enough to be risqué but enough to capture a man's attention. Enough to let them know their gazes were welcome. She was finally emerging from her mourning period and eager to be amongst the living again.

This, fortunately, was well-received when she reached the bottom, and Laurence faded into the background when met with all her admirers. Better still when Joseph bowed at the waist and held out his elbow to her. "Might we make our way to dinner, my lady?"

How much had Laurence told him? Did he know what she'd led his American comrade to believe last night? Best to figure he had.

She curtsied and slipped her arm through his. "Dinner would be lovely, Your Grace."

"Only ever Your Grace when ears are listening," he said out of the corner of his mouth. "Otherwise, I cannot see how we can begin a friendship."

She smiled. "Then how shall I address you?"

"As you did the first time we met." He met her smile. "Joseph, if you would."

While nearly as handsome as Laurence, he regrettably did not have the same effect on her. Where his uncouth friend warmed her in alarming ways when he was close and fired her temper and sense of unease wherever he might be, Joseph felt more like a safe harbor.

"Joseph, it is." She smiled at others in passing but remained most serious with him. "I do apologize for last night. Apologize if I seemed anything but what I am."

"And what is that, Lady Somerset?"

"Abby, if you please."

"Abby, it is." He perked an eyebrow. "What were you last night, other than yourself?"

The way he looked at her told her he understood her actions more than she anticipated. Told her that he, too, might have been trying to escape if for but a night. "So, you understand?"

"More than you can imagine."

Although tempted to ask him to elaborate as she sensed he was a great mystery indeed, they had entered the dining room, and food was being served, including turtle soup, followed by roasted pork and vegetables in a rich butter sauce. Thankfully, Joseph sat beside her. Unfortunately, even though Laurence did not sit near them, he was across the way but still close enough to watch her in that unnerving, all-knowing way of his.

Determined to ignore him, she focused on the lovely entrees and the men around her. Most especially Joseph, of course, as they seemed well-matched from the start. While properly flirtatious, he understood the aristocracy enough to play along where Laurence clearly did not. So said him, challenging any topic of conversation he did not agree with. Yet all the while, he eyed her with a strange mix of amusement and approval rather than desire or even ownership, as she might have expected, given his stunt earlier.

"I must say, your American friend is too forward by half," she remarked after dinner, content to remain on Joseph's arm while still tossing passing men winning smiles. "Does he not realize how offensive he is to those he confronts in conversation?"

"He counts on it," Joseph divulged. "I am convinced that is

half the key to his success."

"Only half?" She narrowed an eye. "And forgive me if I am wrong, but did he not inherit his fortune, hence being an heir?"

She had thought Laurence would have engaged her by now to mock, tease, or flirt, but he had not. Rather, she felt his gaze on her rather than saw it at this point. Knew he watched closely without having any proof of it.

"Laurence did inherit a great deal of wealth," Joseph concurred. "But I rarely see evidence of it, in general. Rather, he prefers building his own empire and challenging people until he filters out everyone but those worth doing business with. Those he knows will be a sure thing."

"Is that what he is doing tonight, then?" She frowned. "Amongst Scottish and English aristocrats, no less?"

He eyed her with amusement. "I think it a bit of this and that."

"Meaning what?"

"Meaning he challenges you every bit as much as he challenges them."

"He is not." Yet he was, and in such an unusual way, she had no idea what to make of it.

Joseph seemed to sense it too. "Are you quite sure?"

She was not sure of anything when it came to Laurence. "Do you mean to say he manipulates me by keeping his distance?"

"It is a distinct possibility, as he is notorious for keeping people guessing about his intentions," he revealed. "Yet make no mistake, it's not personal as Laurence manipulates everyone as a means to his end." He shrugged, yet his tone was affectionate, regardless. "That does not make him unredeemable, though, nor does it stop those who love him from standing by him no matter what."

"You make him sound like a rather closeted monster," she said, deciding to be blunt. "Which, I must admit, makes me distressed I ever met him."

"A closeted monster?" Joseph laughed. "Rest assured, our

American friend is anything *but* that in the circles that matter most to him. Rather, some might call him a pioneer."

"How cliché, given his nationality," she muttered, ignoring her stubbornly relentless curiosity about the obtrusive, crass, overly flirtatious man. "But enough of him. Tell me more about yourself, Joseph. Forgive me, but I know little about the Irish peerage or your family name."

So, he shared, and they spent a lovely few hours together playing cards rather than dancing. All the while, Laurence was in the same room but never close. Never part of the same conversations. Instead, he seemed a conversation away, forever throwing something out there that sparked lively debates and challenged everyone's way of thinking.

More than that, he inevitably drew every female's eye his way. If not because of how irritatingly handsome he was in his evening finery, then for how he paid just enough attention to them. Without a doubt, he made them feel special without somehow managing to irritate their husbands. As to the eligible women in the room, they seemed pitifully smitten with their doe-eyed glances and overly zestful, flirtatious fans.

"They have no idea," she eventually said under her breath. "No clue at all."

Clearly following her random thought, Joseph shook his head. "I am not sure how to put this delicately, my lady—" yet he made things clear with a look that both put her on the defense and made her skin warm at the same time—"but *you* have no idea. Not when you are the woman he wants. And not once in our long years of knowing one another have I ever seen Laurence not get exactly what he desires."

Chapter Four

WHILE LAURENCE WOULD have preferred climbing onto Abby's balcony and ravishing her right where she stood, that had never been his intention. Rather, he'd wanted to draw her out of her room and achieved such, only to find her not drably clothed as he had expected—given his ultimatum—but dressed vibrantly. So beautifully and with such defiant sensuality, it took everything in him not to stare at her the entire night.

Truthfully, he could not decide which version of her with which he was more taken. She who dressed plainly in the tavern, the defiant woman with her long, curly, wild auburn hair blowing in the wind on a balcony, or this sumptuous, almost painfully beautiful version. She seemed to be three different women, and he wanted to possess them all.

Make deep, passionate, *endless* love to every single one.

Not prone to jealousy but rather glad to see Abby as alive in this crowd as she had been among commoners, he felt no need to sweep her off her feet when she left Blake's arm and sauntered down the stairs. Nor did he feel the need to plow through the crowd and deny her Joseph's arm and admiration.

Instead, he bided his time because they had plenty of it. Or at least as much as Abby would need to realize she had wanted to be Laurence's ever since they had bumped into one another. What that might entail in the meantime was open to debate but having her on his arm and in his bed—eventually—would be a good place to start. An essential part.

On his arm, to open doors, of course.

In his bed, because he was no fool.

"Will we not share at least a few words before the evening ends?" he said softly, when they were at last left alone at a card table toward the end of the night. He had watched her flirt endlessly with Joseph, but he'd supposed that was better than watching her pay too much attention to all these other simpering fools.

"Is that so necessary?" She did not shy away but looked at him directly, her expression rather bland. "Have I not done what you asked, by being down here?" Her tone was mocking. Borderline callous. "Am I not properly a puppet on your strings?"

"No more than I was last night on yours," he cut back, suddenly frustrated and thinking with his cock when that was something he never did. In his position, thinking below the waist could be his ruin. That aside, his words and viewpoint were wrong, and he knew it, so he fixed it. "You are very much your own woman, Abby. What happened tonight will not happen again." Then, because he could not help himself and had to win, he said, "How could it when I will not need to beg you once more?" He dropped his voice and made things clear. "Next time, *every* time, you will come down those stairs without me having to say a word."

"Only a mere word?" she quipped dryly. "When you are so very good with rocks?"

"Pebbles, darling." He could not help a chuckle. "Nothing more. Nothing less."

"Rocks, vines, and blackmail," she said through clenched teeth. "All childish behavior, to say the least."

He shrugged and pointed out the obvious. "Yet, effective."

However much she might dislike him, and as much as he equally loathed relying on blackmail of all things, it had worked earlier, and she'd finally emerged from a room he knew had caused her a great deal of pain. She'd broken free, even if at his whim, of old habits and a chamber she had spent numerous nights in, seeing to an old, obstinate man's needs.

"Such arrogance," she exclaimed, not charmed by his methods. "Who do you think you are?"

If only he knew. Best answer? What his father had made him.

He had no chance to answer before the others rejoined them, and it was probably for the best, lest he gave her an answer she would not much like. One he would probably not like either, even if it would be the truth.

Even though he was tempted to pull Abby into a darkened corner before she retired that night to show her what it could be like between them, he knew better. He had pushed her past mildly flattered to downright appalled for no other reason than her denial of how attracted they were to each other.

"And you do see it just like that, don't you?" Joseph marveled the next day when Laurence muttered that while he would most certainly make Abby his, the timeline might be a tad longer than he'd originally anticipated. "You imagine the games you play with a woman more wounded than you think will have her falling into your arms?"

"I had rather hoped." Yet he was starting to see the error of his ways. "Truth told, I might have underestimated just how much work I would be facing."

"*Work?*" Joseph sipped his whisky and shook his head. "Do you hear yourself? Abby is a living, breathing woman who deserves more than a lad who sees her as *work*."

"Did you misunderstand my purpose in taking an English aristocratic wife?" He might not like where things stood between him and Abby, but he had been clear with Joseph from the start. Love was and never had been his intention. Yes, he could admit to wanting to lie with Abby, especially considering he'd thought an English wife would be stiff and terribly boring, but love was never a factor. Affection, perhaps, but nothing more genuine. "This *is* work. Lady Abigail is work and nothing more. She is a means to an end."

"I rarely say this, but you do not represent your countrymen well right now, Laurence."

"Nor did I intend to." Laurence downed the rest of his drink and set aside his glass. "The goal was only ever to outdo my countrymen, *old chap*." He considered Joseph. "Should I assume we are still in competition after last night? You *did* seem quite taken with her."

"I found her company entertaining," Joseph replied vaguely. "But I cannot say if we got on well enough to warrant a full-out battle with you which could get rather tiresome."

"And here I thought the opposite." He grinned and shook his head. "Don't give up so quickly, friend. I mean to take my time about it."

"I will believe that when I see it." Joseph eyed him with amusement. "So, you intend to court her properly then?"

"I'm not sure how proper it will be." He quirked the corner of his mouth. "But yes, I think her best won over in a few weeks rather than a few days."

"Only a few *weeks*?" Joseph shook his head and grinned. "I think you overestimate your charm when it comes to Lady Abigail, my friend."

"Doubtful." He recalled the telling heat that had simmered between them at the tavern. "She just needs thawing out from her last marriage to better enjoy the finer things in life."

Joseph snorted. "And those finer things would be you?"

Him and only ever him. "Need you ask?"

DECISION MADE, LAURENCE realized he just needed to cross paths with her as much as possible. Something that happened sooner rather than later when he and Joseph returned from a fox hunt later that day. She was standing in the great hall with a host of newcomers.

"Ah, there you two are." Maude waved them over and introduced everyone before squeezing the hand of a lovely woman with pale blond hair. "And this is my dear friend, Lady Stanton."

He could not help but note how the lady's gaze lingered on Joseph before she curtsied to them both. Meanwhile, Abby did her best to seem oblivious to Laurence's presence as she smiled at the gentleman who stood with Lady Stanton—or Isabella, as he would learn later from Harold. Sister to Margaret, she was widowed and one of Abby's dearest friends.

Needless to say, Abby locked elbows with Isabella, flirted shamelessly with her admirers, and yet again went her own way without a backward glance. And so, the chase began anew and out in the open rather than holed up in her room or on her *freedom balcony* as he'd heard she had coined it over the years. According to Harold, it was with good reason, too, considering the rantings and ravings servants had heard coming from her late husband. It seemed he'd been forever in a foul mood, and Abby had taken the brunt of it.

While tempted to shove past all this game-playing and take her aside so they might talk, he knew better than to think she would trust him with a heartfelt conversation, a means, of course, to win over her trust and heart. He suspected that might be his only course of action. Regrettably, he had no idea how to do that. However, he knew how to keep her drawn to him, and that, based on the previous night, was to flirt as shamelessly with other women as she did with other men.

He must keep her feeling new emotions rather than allowing her to focus too much on the ones behind her. There would be time for all that later if there were no way around it. Hopefully, there was a way, however, because he preferred that she simply forget her late husband ever existed. Start anew with him and leave the past behind.

Might that day come sooner rather than later, too, because, despite flirting with various lovely women, they were not Abby.

None possessed the same provocative flare nor the sultry light in their eyes that came so naturally to her. She had a way of drawing men's eyes. Gazes that undoubtedly envisioned her writhing in pleasure beneath them.

He caught her glancing his way several times in irritation when one woman or another laughed at something he'd said, but unlike Abby, who tossed her head back and laughed gaily at what one bloke or another said, their amusement rang false. Her laughter was sensually genuine in a way that only seemed to enamor her admirers further, and he did not blame them.

"It is said Lady Somerset was highly sought after during her coming-out ball years ago," Harold reported as he helped Laurence prepare for dinner that evening. "That Lord Somerset was most despised for claiming her as his own."

"Could he claim her that easily, then?" *If so, how had he gone about it?*

"He could indeed because his family's name was old and not to be ignored." Harold shook his head. "Most certainly not by the daughter of a mere baron. Rumor has it her father gave her no choice once Lord Somerset made his intentions known, which was straight away." He frowned. "She was not even given the chance to dance with another. Not during her coming-out ball and certainly not at any ball to follow."

"Truly?" He met his man's frown. "All things considered, I would have thought her a mouse of a woman by now, her spirit withered away, but she is quite vivacious instead."

"I agree one would think her more subdued, yet…"

"What is it?" he prompted when his valet seemed undecided if he should go on.

"I am not sure I should say."

"Yet it is clearly common knowledge, or you would not know it."

"Even so." Harold notched his chin in defiance. "I need not repeat it."

"Yet you will because I paid you." While tempted to remind

him of his potential elevated status, he sensed his valet's pride might get in the way. So, he offered reassurances instead. "I will not repeat what you say if that makes any difference. Nor do I intend to repeat anything you tell me, in general."

At least not to anyone but Abby if it served his purpose.

"So you will not tell anyone this?" Harold asked tentatively.

"You have my word."

"Are you quite sure?"

"I would not have said it otherwise."

Harold considered him for another moment before he finally nodded and shared. "Well, it seems many below stairs feel there are two sides to Lady Somerset," his man divulged softly, even though they were alone. "That which she shows everyone and then another, far more somber one."

He found that hard to believe. "Why do they think such?"

"Because she was overheard on more than one occasion weeping on her balcony when she and her late husband visited."

"Although unfortunate, that is not overly shocking, considering her lot in life." He shrugged. "I doubt she weeps nowadays."

"One would think, but not that long ago, a maid under her employee said her tears have been quite recent as well," Harold said. "She presents one picture around others but grows quite sad when she is alone."

"That *is* rather personal." And he was put off by it, for her sake. Frustrated that such talk abounded below stairs. "Do you think she's still grieving?"

He knew little of how aristocratic women thought but sensed Abby would be mortified to know this information. In addition, he highly doubted it was grief over her late husband. If so, what a waste of tears.

"Perhaps she still grieves, but it is doubtful." Harold sighed. "Rumor has it she has been that way for years. Since the moment she first married Lord Somerset."

Somehow that did not surprise him. If anything, it made him angrier still at a man he had never met. While older men married younger women all the time, most did not have such a sizeable age gap.

"What do they say about Lord Somerset below stairs?"

"Other than he was arrogant and unpleasant to staff, very little."

"So, he did not beat her?" Because he would reach into the bastard's grave and strangle him until he was deader than he already was if he had.

"I have not heard such." Distress flared in Harold's light brown eyes. "I can only hope not."

He could not agree more. "Is there anything else I should know?"

"Actually, there *is* one more small thing of interest." Harold looked Laurence's attire over and nodded with approval. "It seems Lord and Lady MacLauchlin have started to coin certain balls here as *second-chance balls*. Dances with the sole purpose of bringing love matches together. According to rumor, it seems tomorrow night's ball is just that." His eyebrows edged up. "Hence, as you might have noticed, it is the reason why there are so many eligible bachelors close to Lady Somerset's age already in attendance."

"I have noticed," he muttered. While he was aware Blake and Maude were playing matchmakers again, he had not realized they were having one of their infamous balls so soon. He took in Harold's unimpressed look. "Why do you seem so put off by it?"

"Because of the various bets being hedged both below and above stairs."

He did not like the sound of that. "Over what?"

"Even though this ball is being thrown, however discreetly, so Lady Somerset might, at last, enjoy what has long been lost to her, some say it's counterproductive." Harold shrugged. "After all, it is said Lady Somerset will not dance. That after years of having to dance solely with such a possessive man, she sees it as a threshold she will not cross again."

"How interesting." He gave that some thought before he

grinned. "And no doubt it's something I can use to my advantage."

"So you will convince her to dance with you?"

"One way or another, I will, my friend." He clasped Harold's shoulder in passing and laughed. "Indeed, I will."

He'd thought it odd that he had not seen Abby dance yet, as she had surely been asked. Now he understood why, and it could not work out more perfectly for him. Or her, he hoped, as it rather sounded like a bridge she needed to cross.

⇤⇥

"I CANNOT SAY I much trust that look on your face," Joseph commented later that evening as they enjoyed a glass of brandy after dinner. They had a perfect view of the ladies playing cards. Specifically Abby and Isabella. "You are eyeing Lady Somerset as though you have a trick up your sleeve."

"Am I that obvious?" Because he could just as easily be eyeing her for her stunning beauty. As usual, she was impossible to look away from.

"You have been obvious enough to pull a wary glance or two from her this evening." Joseph's gaze narrowed on him. "What are you doing to that poor woman, Laurence? Because I suspect you hold some sort of sway over her that..." He trailed off and narrowed his eyes even further when the truth occurred to him. "Tell me you are not doing what I think you are? That you are not holding her prisoner under the threat of unsavory gossip?"

"Then I will not tell you that." He shrugged and sipped his drink. "Even though I very much am."

"Bloody hell, man." Joseph shook his head. "That's low, even for you."

"You know I don't always play fair when I want something." He gave his friend a pointed look. "Why would I stop now when I want her above all?"

Laurence knew how that sounded the moment he said it, but he meant it. He wanted Abby with a fierceness that grew by the day. By the very hour.

"By God," Joseph murmured, eyeing him in shock. "I have never seen this side of you." He shook his head. "Honestly, I did not think you had it in you."

"Whatever do you mean?" he said warily because he suspected they were no longer talking about his sometimes ruthless business nature.

"I mean, I did not think you could feel genuine affection for a woman." An annoying smirk hovered on Joseph's mouth. "Yet somehow, despite having known Abby for so little time and hardly speaking with her to the best of my knowledge, you have fallen quite hard. Thinking beyond your cock, to be sure."

"You could not be more wrong." *Right*? Because he would not know otherwise in such unfamiliar territory. "While yes, I certainly desire her—what fool would not?—rest assured she remains a means to an end. A very lucrative end, at that."

"So you say." Clearly marveling at the situation, Joseph chuckled. "Which should make this whole affair much more entertaining to watch."

"Not an affair," he clarified. "But a marriage to an aristocrat, which in turn would open doors to me and my businesses."

To that end, he would put the next phase of his plan in motion that very night.

Chapter Five

"I MUST SAY you look remarkably lovely, my friend," Isabella praised as they stood on Abby's balcony and enjoyed a glass of wine before dinner. Despite the chill, her friend knew she liked it out here, so she had not hesitated to join her. "There is a new light in your eyes I have not seen before, and I cannot help but wonder if it has anything to do with your dashing American."

She had told Isabella everything about her predicament with Laurence from start to finish.

"He is not mine and most certainly not dashing." She frowned. "How can you say such nonsense after everything I just told you about the scoundrel?"

"Because there is a new light in your eyes," Isabella repeated. A small, knowing smile hovered on her lips. "One that tells me that however opposed you may be to your scoundrel, he has most certainly caught your attention."

"Clearly." She pointed at the vine running alongside her balcony. "On that through blackmail, no less." In truth, he was worse than a scoundrel. "He is utterly shameless and, I dare say, cruel, taking advantage of a woman just out of mourning. A proper gentleman would have respected my need for privacy."

"Indeed, a proper gentleman would have," Isabella agreed. "So it's a good thing he is not."

She was surprised to hear her friend compliment him, the

cad. Handsome, yes, intriguing, certainly. But to say his boorish, blackmailing behavior was good? Absolutely not.

"You cannot mean to defend him," she exclaimed. "His actions have been barbaric thus far."

"Yet admittedly exciting." Isabella peered down the length of the vine. "You said he nearly made it all the way up? That takes a certain level of strength, does it not?" She slid a rather saucy smile Abby's way. "But then, he *did* appear quite fit, not to mention incredibly handsome, in case you had not noticed."

She had, and her friend very well knew it. "What does handsome have to do with his ability to climb a vine?"

"I would say the latter only accentuated the former when he nearly made it to your ledge." Isabella chuckled and shrugged. "Not that his winning good looks kept him free of projectiles." She outright laughed. "Did you *really* throw things at him when he was in such a precarious position?"

"I did, and I would again," she assured. "When one does something so foolish, one must be willing to accept the repercussions, no matter dire they may be."

"How dire, to be sure," Isabella murmured, growing rather serious. "Tell me, darling, how are you truly doing outside of your exciting new American adventure? It worries me that you decided to stay in this room." She frowned from said room to Abby. "You realize there are balconies off other chambers? That you might have at last stayed in one of the rooms higher up?"

"I know." She sighed and shook her head. "I wish I could tell you why I stayed in this room again. I suppose it just felt like the right thing to do since it's my first visit without Reginald."

"I see." Yet Isabella appeared dubious and concerned. "I do hope you will change your mind soon so we might enjoy a better view." She grew amused when her gaze roamed to the vine again. "Besides, seeing how high your scoundrel can climb might be fun."

Or terrifying, but she certainly did not voice that.

"Enough about me." Abby joined Isabella at the railing and

sipped her wine. "How are you?"

"I confess that I'm as glad as you to be free of my mourning period," she said. "I will miss the easy relationship my late husband and I shared but, as you know, little more."

Isabella's husband had been a dull sort, indeed. According to her, he had possessed no real interests, including his wife. Intimacy had been a necessary chore and excitement of any sort lacking in their marriage. All in all, Isabella had thought him remarkably boring, but at least they had been the same age.

"I also must confess," Isabella went on, "that I look forward to spending time at your second-chance ball tomorrow and enjoying all these eligible bachelors that have no chance with you. Especially that Irish duke. Though I do hope he is as daring as he is handsome, for I cannot deal with another dull aristocratic man with no zest for life. Or zest for *me*, for that matter." She tilted her head and went on before Abby could respond. "Speaking of the ball your sister is planning, she does recall you do not dance these days, yes? That you have sworn it off?"

"She does, yet still seems to think this ball of bachelors will change my mind." Maude was certainly a wishful thinker this time. "Yet I fear it will not because I have no desire to dance with any man ever again."

Something she suspected Laurence did not know, given how he ended up eyeing her throughout the night whenever talk of the ball came up. She felt like a tasty appetizer under a predator's appraisal. He had switched modes from the previous evening, making his desire for her far more obvious to others despite barely speaking with her. One thing was certain, though.

He was up to no good.

She was positive of it.

Even now, she could feel his gaze on her from across the room. Feel how he bided his time before he pounced. Because he was getting ready to do just that with what she imagined was another indecent proposal or threat. And while she dreaded it, frustratingly enough, she was also a tad excited. Curious to see what atrocious thing he might do next.

AS IT HAPPENED, she should have gone with dread over excitement when he finally made his move later that evening.

"If you would take a stroll with me, Lady Somerset?" Laurence held out the crook of his arm and dared her to say no with his eyes. "I would so enjoy your company."

She could just imagine.

"What is it?" she muttered after they turned down a candlelit hallway and were out of earshot. "Because I assume you are getting ready to offend me once more."

"Was I so offensive before?"

"Very."

"Then you have my apologies."

"Somehow, I doubt that."

"Yet you do." He steered her down another hallway, this one with far fewer people. "The last thing I wish to do is offend you, Abby." His voice deepened like it had at the tavern when they stood so close, and his desire became palpable. "Rather, I would much prefer to do the opposite."

The way he looked at her made clear his true intentions. Based on how her skin warmed and breathing became more difficult, it also made clear that he would not be easy to stave off if he set his mind to it. More specifically, she would have a problem if he behaved anywhere near as he had at the tavern. Because whether she was ultimately embarrassed or not, his proximity and how she'd felt when he merely touched her hand ignited all sorts of foreign and far too pleasurable sensations.

"What did you want to talk to me about, Mr. Wright?" she said, keeping things professional.

"Call me Laurence."

"No."

"I insist."

"And if I do not?"

"I will be most disappointed."

"How disappointed?"

"More than I think you would appreciate."

"So, it is to be blackmail until the very end with you, is it not?" She stopped walking and crossed her arms over her chest rather than touch him a moment longer. "If that is the case, then why not demand I become your wife now rather than play these foolish games?"

"I considered it, as I have no intention of letting you go." His gaze lingered on her face as though he could not get enough of her. "But I find I would prefer this to be a mutual decision. That you will want to become my wife the day we marry."

"Then I fear your battle lost before it has begun." She shook her head. "Because I will not marry again, let alone wed a foreigner."

"Why?"

"Why to which?"

"Both."

"If you must know, I will not imprison myself in another marriage when I have the finances and status to remain widowed." She was not quite sure how to put the second part of her answer other than to be truthful. "As to marrying a foreigner, it is quite simple. I have no desire to leave England nor my sisters."

"While I believe the first part, I do not, for a moment, believe the entirety of the second part." He seemed to gaze straight into her soul. "Rather, while I'm sure you want to remain close to your sisters, you also long to see and go everywhere you can. Without a doubt, you crave experiencing a world you have only ever dreamt of."

Did she ever, but he need not know that. "And I can do that without remarrying."

"You can," he granted. "But it costs to travel. While I imagine you are wealthy enough, I do not suspect, having only a portion of your late husband's estate, that you can afford to go many places while still maintaining a residence here."

"So now you think to lure me with your wealth?"

"Is it working?"

"Not in the least." Although it did have its appeal. *Nevertheless.* "I will not be bought, Mr. Wright."

When the corner of his mouth curled up and he stepped closer, those heated moments in the tavern came rushing back. "Are you quite sure, Abby?" He ran his fingers down her arm so lightly, her head swam. "Because, as you know, there is no amount I would not pay. No place I would not take you. No country I would not show you."

Once upon a time, she would have given anything to experience all that. To experience *him.* But her ability to choose for herself had been taken away, first by her father, and then by her husband. She would never allow herself—or her choices—to be controlled by a man, again.

"Yet all the freedom you offer comes at too high a price." She stiffened her legs when her knees weakened at the feel of him. "One I shall never be willing to pay again."

"Does my proposal sound like such a prison, then?" He shook his head. "Because I would never hold you back from doing what you wanted to do. Rather I would prefer to see the opposite. Prefer to watch you flourish in a life that should have been yours from the beginning."

"Such sweet words from a blackmailer who I doubt has ever been denied a thing, be it from a woman or otherwise."

"Very true," he confirmed. "True because I'm relentless when I set my mind to something." Once again, he was ruthlessly confident. "While I confess, I have never applied my business methods to a woman, I cannot imagine failing."

"Though you very much should." Unconvinced he had not pursued other women to this degree, she gave him a pointed look. "Moreover, I recommend you continue your pursuit by being honest."

"Did I say something that struck you as false?"

Not so much false as suspect. "Why me?" she said. "Why me when I suspect you have wanted other women? When marrying a fellow American would be far more practical?"

"If I wanted a woman, I bedded her, not married her," he said, without blinking. "As to marrying an Englishwoman instead of an American, my initial reason was to become part of your aristocracy via matrimony to open doors to my businesses that are otherwise shut." He trailed his fingers back up her arm. "Then I met you."

Dear Lord, he was painfully blunt and offensively so. Something only made worse by how horribly aware of his touch she was. How he could somehow make her hate and crave him all at once.

"Indeed, you *did* meet me." She frowned. "And you thought me a trollop, which makes me pity the aristocrat you would have eventually pursued."

"Why, because I enjoyed female companionship prior to meeting her?" He stepped closer still, too close, yet she could not seem to back up. "Female companionship from a woman I most certainly would have made my mistress?"

"Good *God*." She rounded her eyes and finally found the strength to step away. "And you thought I would have agreed to that?"

"Considering you were a trollop who would have been well provided for, I did." His gaze roamed over her like it had when he'd thought her said *trollop*, and he stepped close again, forcing her to take another step back. "Fortunately, and quite luckily for me, it turns out you are exactly what I want in more ways than one."

"You truly have no idea how to court a potential wife, do you?" She shook her head, baffled by him. "Laurence, you do realize you just told the woman you wish to marry that you would think nothing of taking a mistress? A woman more impossible to convince than most as is?"

"*Ah.*" He issued one of those rarely seen, charming grins that made her breath catch. "I *knew* it was only a matter of time before you used my name."

She had, hadn't she? *Abby, you're such a fool,* she told herself. She'd let her natural, pleasant personality rule her mouth and had given him more fuel for his fire.

Laurence took another step, and she retreated, until her back hit the wall. He rested his hand beside her head and stepped dauntingly close this time. So close she became overly aware of how his broad shoulders caged her in. More so, she became far too aware of his effect on her, from the sudden sensitivity of her breasts to the dull ache blossoming between her thighs. A feeling that caught her off guard because she had never experienced it before.

"I never make promises I cannot keep when going into business with someone," he went on softly, his warm breath fanning her cheek. "Therefore, I promise you with every fiber of my being that I will never take a mistress if you become my wife." He grazed the side of her neck with the back of his fingers, making it hard to think. "How could I when I know you will more than satisfy me?" His voice grew husky. "How well we will satisfy each other?"

She struggled to find her voice and focus, yet everything but his touch faded away. There was nothing but his lips, hovering next to hers. The potent aroma of his spicy masculine scent. His heat, which somehow pulsed through her even though they did not touch. She discovered she'd begun holding her breath at some point. And stopped thinking altogether when he leaned in as though he were going to kiss her but murmured in her ear instead.

"That said, I would like to propose something to you, Abby." He seemed to inhale the scent of her hair before his gaze returned to her face. "A contract, if you will, that says that, in return for two things, I will walk away without ever revealing your clandestine behavior at the tavern. I will stop pursuing your hand in marriage and never look back, or I will be in breach of contract."

Again, she tried to speak but to no avail. So, she cleared her throat and tried once more, grateful her voice somewhat worked this time. "You cannot be serious." Already seeing a flaw in his plan, she narrowed her eyes. "Outside of a marriage registry, a woman cannot sign a contract with a man. And while you are clearly an unusual thinker, I do not doubt those same rules also apply in America."

"Yet a contract shall be written up by me and signed by both of us in front of a witness of our choosing."

"And therein lies the catch." She sidled away before he touched her again, and she gave in to his every wish. "It would not be binding because I am a mere woman with few legal rights."

"Yet I would honor it because I do not betray my contracts," he vowed, his tone different all of a sudden. Quite serious, indeed. "They are what makes me who I am. All I have. My very worth." He shook his head, not flirtatious in the least now. "And that, Lady Abigail, is something I refuse to betray, even for you."

She was surprised by how his words saddened her for no other reason than he meant them. This was what his work had done to him. While he was friends with Blake and Joseph, they were likely the only few he had outside of business. How else could it be when he thought his profession was the only thing that made him worthy?

Walk away now, she preached to herself. *Walk away, and let him say what he would about her, be damned the repercussions.* Yet her feet felt part of the floor, and her curiosity was piqued despite how lewd his proposal would likely be.

"What are these two things you want from me?" she said before she could stop herself.

"First, that you teach me how to waltz," he said, surprising her. "Second, that you travel with me anywhere that requires you stepping foot on a boat."

She waited for him to go on and request that she lay with him out of wedlock, no matter how scandalous, but he did not. Instead, he simply waited for an answer.

"That is it?" Though neither was necessarily a small request. "Really?" She narrowed her eyes again. "Because I find it hard to believe you do not already know how to waltz."

"Yet I do not." He shrugged. "I meant to make the time before pursuing an aristocratic wife but, alas, never got around to it."

"And now you want me to teach you." She frowned when it occurred to her that Maude might very well factor into his bizarre request. It made perfect sense, given Laurence was so driven when he fancied something. Not to mention perceptive. "You want me to teach you to waltz despite having not seen me waltz once? Despite having not seen me participate in any sort of dancing, for that matter? This might very well imply I do not know how."

"I might not be able to waltz, but I do know it would have been one of the first things you learned for your coming-out ball." He held out his elbow and prompted her to continue strolling with him. "More than that, I have made a point of learning about you, Abby. So I know you have not danced with anyone since Lord Somerset. That you refuse to."

While it unsettled her that he'd sought information about her, it made sense. Fit into the mold of someone who dealt in business ventures. Most certainly fit into the mold of how relentless he seemed.

"You understand I will not teach you in the ballroom around others," she said, thinking about it. Although the idea of such intimacy with him was dangerous, a small part of her wondered what it might feel like. She had enjoyed waltzing during her lessons as a girl but had found it daunting with Reginald. Not nearly the romantic dream she'd envisioned. "I have your word that wherever I teach you will be most discreet?"

He grinned. "I was counting on it."

But, of course, he was. "This has nothing to do with waltzing, does it?" She should have known better. "It is but a means to seduce me."

"I imagine partly, as I do so enjoy it." His grin only grew before he relented. "But no, Abby, if you do not want it to be anything but lessons, rest assured, that is precisely what it will be."

Even though she sensed he meant it, he could just as easily turn it into something more. Something that she suspected would far outdo the simple pleasure of a waltz.

"You understand this does not make you a cut above the other gentleman pursuing me, nor does it make you my exclusive dance partner?" Even though she suspected it would. "That teaching you does not mean I might not choose to dance with others tomorrow night?"

"But of course." Yet he sounded confidently dubious. "I would never hold you back from finding bliss in another's arms, love."

"Abby."

He offered one of those heart-stopping, dimple-ridden smiles of his. "For now."

"Always, or we have no deal." Because the thought of loving a man like him was more than a little daunting. It would be as unpredictable and risky as riding in a carriage on sheer ice.

"So, you agree to my terms otherwise?" His smile only broadened. "Both of them?"

Did she? Should she? Both were huge leaps with equally precarious outcomes if she were not careful and did not mind her heart. Because she was not foolish enough to think Laurence could not conquer it as mightily as he conquered everything else. So, was this really such a good idea? Was she even remotely equipped to handle a man like him? Able to stand strong and remember that she must maintain her freedom no matter what?

"I need time to think about it," she said before she realized that was not true. Not at all. This was a chance to stand on her own two feet and prove to a man once and for all that he did not control her. Own her. More pointedly, to prove to herself that she could overcome anything a man tried to throw at her. So may Laurence try his very best because she intended to see him fail. "Actually, on second thought, I do not need time to think about it, after all."

Chapter Six

LAURENCE HAD COUNTED on feeling a sense of triumph when Abby accepted his proposal but did not expect to feel so pleased nor relieved as he lay in bed later that night. Nor did he anticipate the rush he felt at the headway they had made earlier.

Headway of which he fully intended to take advantage.

He already knew how he would handle their waltzing lessons, but what of their journey to another country? Which one would she choose? What would she think of sailing for the first time? He longed to see her expression if she enjoyed it. Longed to see the shimmer of excitement in her luminous eyes he did not doubt would be there.

A similar sort of excitement he imagined seeing when they finally made love. Because, married or not, that *would* happen. It was inevitable. And what they experienced that first time would nourish and cultivate their bond until she craved only him. He'd never been so driven to do anything, and that goal had only intensified after being with her earlier.

After touching her soft, slender neck and inhaling the scent of her silky, sweet hair.

Everything about her drove him to distraction, and he wanted more. *So* much more. He wanted to hear her soft moans when he took her and drown in her cries when he brought her to her peak. Hear her beg for more because she could not get enough.

It might not happen right away, but it would happen soon enough; he wasn't just determined to marry her but properly seduce her. Own her flesh in the best way possible. And he would continue the battle toward that goal the next night prior to the ball when he requested lessons before she went downstairs.

Lessons he much anticipated the next day as he and Joseph went riding. Blake would have joined them, but he was too busy overseeing preparations for that evening.

"You seem quite chipper." Joseph eyed him curiously. "Might I assume you have made headway with the lovely Lady Abigail?"

He grinned. "You may, because I did."

When Joseph's eyebrows shot up in surprise, he told him what had transpired and what he'd gotten Abby to agree to.

"Devil's teeth," his friend exclaimed. "I admit that is a great deal more than I would have thought."

"Me too." He tilted his top hat and could not stop grinning. "But, in the end, it seems my lovely lady of the night could not deny me."

"Even though your supposed honesty is built on a lie," Joseph noted. "Of which I suspect she knows nothing as you can, in fact, waltz and well at that."

"Perhaps." He looked at the bright side of his deceit. "In America, that is. These British aristocrats might very well have their own version."

Joseph shook his head. "You do have a way of skirting around things." He considered Laurence in a way that told him he would not like what his friend said next. "To that end, are you sure you want to go into an agreement like this with Abby? A proposal you claim is built on honesty without being entirely truthful up front? Might it not jeopardize your contract going forward if she learns the truth? Worse yet, the trust you are hoping to establish with her?"

"It would if I were not convinced the British have a different variation to their waltz," he reminded.

"So, it is with a white lie in which you choose to begin your life with her." Joseph looked at Laurence in warning. "The fact Abby has agreed to what you presented tells me she is not opposed to trusting you, friend. Adventuring forth with you if only a country over. So, tread carefully because I see how much you care for her already. At the very least, tell her your version of the truth, may that be enough."

"Perhaps," he conceded.

"She was a trapped butterfly for a long time, Laurence." Joseph shook his head. "That said, you should cherish and promote the freedom she no doubt senses with you rather than re-cage her with a half-truth because that is exactly what will happen. She will take even the slightest fib from you as the first of many. More importantly, it will make her disbelieve any sense of freedom within marriage you might have promised her."

"Yet there is so much fun to be had in pretending," he argued, scowling because his friend made good sense. "Ample time she has no choice but to spend with me."

"Perhaps." Joseph shrugged. "Or a great deal of time taken from the life you might have had together if she learns the truth."

"Unless you or Blake tells her, it's doubtful she will ever know." In no mood for Joseph's sometimes overly cautious nature, he waved it off. "So you need not worry."

"It's likely Maude knows as well," Joseph pointed out. "Because I suspect Blake tells his wife everything as they are not just in love but close friends. So therein lies yet another person you need to keep quiet."

Rather than endlessly assure his friend all would be well, he turned the conversation to Joseph himself and put any possibility of losing Abby from his mind.

She was his.

It was all but a done deal.

"I could not help but notice you dancing with Lady Stanton last night. Several times for that matter." He shot his friend a crooked grin. "Might you have your sights set on a possible wife as well?"

"I think our acquaintance too young by far to imagine that." The corners of Joseph's mouth tugged down. "Besides, you know full well that whom I will marry is already decided, whether love is involved or not."

"Ah, so setting Isabella aside, am I to assume your pursuit of Lady Abigail is behind us?"

"As if you did not know that from the start." Joseph tipped his hat in return. "But it was fun letting you believe you had competition for a moment or two."

He grinned. "And it was equally fun letting you think you ever had a chance."

After that, they left talk of women and wives behind and enjoyed their afternoon as more and more guests arrived. So many young, eligible bachelors that it spoke to Abby's appeal because, despite her status and dowry, the count seemed excessive.

"I did tell you Lady Abigail was much admired, sir." Harold smoothed out Laurence's tailcoat that evening and looked him over once more, keen on finding even the slightest hint of a wrinkle. "Not just for her beauty but for her late husband's name."

"Indeed." He counted the minutes to when he could rip her old English name away and make her a Wright. "All the way back to William the Conqueror, at that."

"Precisely." Harold shook his head in awe. "And I cannot blame them as a lineage that old is noteworthy."

"Even though her husband was anything but," he groused. "Have you learned anything more about him? How he was with her?"

"No, but I have heard more about how she was with him their last few years."

"And?" he persisted when Harold hesitated. Where he would have taken any information last night to secure her, now he was hungry for knowledge in a whole new way. In a fashion he could not quite make sense of. He wanted to understand Abby better.

Get to the bottom of every little thing she might be keeping from him.

Learn all her secrets.

He wanted to be prepared for moments like when he told her he knew she disliked dancing. Because, however brief, there had been a flash of pain in her eyes. Pain that showed him what Harold had heard below stairs about her being two different people might be true. So said the sadness and trepidation she'd blinked away almost as soon as it appeared.

An aspect of her he intended to understand no matter what it took.

"It seems there might have been more to Lady Abigail's melancholy," Harold said. "Or so I imagine considering the care in which she attended her late husband when he became crippled."

"I have heard that." He shook his head. "That is nothing new."

"No, but have you heard how caring she actually was?"

"Not specifically, no."

"Well, it seems she might not have been forced to care for Lord Somerset as time went on but genuinely wanted to at the end," Harold said, his tone quite respectful. "While she clearly cared for him in public during his more unfortunate incidents, it seems, according to staff, that it was not all for show. Rather, she was just as caring in private, even going so far as to spend hours reading to him. They claim she might have found a certain love for him and that he was, shockingly enough, kind to her when they were alone. Or rather, kinder than he was to most."

So said a lady's maid who saw to Abby's needs during one of their visits to MacLauchlin Castle when her own maid was suffering from a bout of sickness.

"Are you telling me they..." *What?* He could not even imagine it. "Fell in some sort of love in the end despite all the reasons she should not have loved him? Surely *not*."

"I do not know." Harold shook his head. "Other than to say those I have spoken with claim she changed him in the end. At least in private."

"So an old man tried to find forgiveness during his dying days in the arms of a wife he should never have married to begin with." Laurence saw it for what it was. "And with little choice in the matter, Abby cared for him. That does not speak to love. Not nearly."

He didn't bother waiting for an answer because he knew he was right. How else could it be when Abby had been forced into a stuffy, unforgiving aristocratic marriage? Surely, whatever the gossip, it was wrong in this regard. He left his room, still musing about this new information.

The musicians downstairs had just started playing, so he made his way out back and around the castle, ready to take advantage of the first part of his plan.

Despite what Joseph had advised, having Abby teach him the waltz was the best way to force her into his arms and show her everything she had been missing. Because he would catch on to her dancing lessons just enough that she would be helpless to leave his embrace or desire to go downstairs to this second-chance ball, as it were.

To this masquerade of ill-intentioned suitors who only wanted her for superficial reasons.

Eager to make her realize she need only have eyes for him tonight, he grabbed hold of the vine beneath her balcony but froze when he heard something unsettling from above. What *was* that? Concerned, he climbed just enough and cocked his head, straining to hear, only to realize it was a woman weeping.

More specifically, Abby weeping.

Worried about her, he kept climbing, only to slow when he heard Maude's voice.

"Oh, dear sister, there you are." He heard movement above as though Maude went to Abby. "What is it, darling?"

Abby responded, but it was impossible to make out her words. Nor could he hear Maude's response, as the two must have gone inside.

Unsure what to do, he climbed back down and leaned against the castle wall. He had planned things perfectly, but now his thoughts were scattered. They were going in every direction when that never happened to him. Thinking clearly was his strong suit. What he did best.

Yet at the moment, he could not form a solid, logical thought.

He raked his hand through his hair and stared at the clouds racing past the moon. Tried to figure out what his next move should be. Had Abby truly loved her late husband? If so, what was he to make of that? Truth told, his confidence in making her his had been dependent on him seducing her and showing her what she'd long deserved to feel. Or at least what he'd thought she'd never had the opportunity to feel.

Would that still have the same impact if she had actually *loved* Reginald? If she suffered that elusive emotion that seemed to hold a great deal of sway over others? The only emotion he had ever seen overcome good logic.

Yet, like any emotion, it was one he could work with.

One he *had* to work with if it meant securing their marriage and keeping Abby in his life. He frowned, shook his head, and revised that thought. If it meant a way into the peerage. A means to expand his businesses. As his father would have counseled, he focused on that thought for a few minutes until he was back on track.

"Never let anything get in the way of your goals and expanding our empire, son," his father had said. "All that matters is being better and superseding all who mean to challenge you." He had pointed from his chest to his forehead. "You think not with your heart but with your head. Do you understand? Only ever your head because that is the only thing you can trust. The only thing that will make you better than all the rest in life."

He nodded and inhaled deeply. His father had been right, and Laurence had proven it time and time again. The best way to beat them all was to remain unattached and driven. Never fall victim to affairs of the heart. So he must remember, no matter how much he wanted to bed Abby, she was a means to an end.

Yes, he would sink into her welcoming heat, but that was it. Nothing more. He would give her the adventures she craved, and she would do the same for him with her lovely body. Over and over until they tired of one another just as his mother had tired of his father and turned to another.

He closed his eyes and set aside what that had entailed for him. How unfailingly strict his life had become afterward. Instead, he breathed deeply, visualized how he should go about things now, and only came to one conclusion. With the same confidence, he had handled everything thus far.

Confidence that had been second nature to him up until the day he laid eyes on Abby.

Rather than dwell on that fact, he squared his shoulders, headed back inside, and spoke with Blake. Having written up a few contracts for different possible scenarios, he let his friend know which contract applied to Laurence and Abby now, then waited for her to come down. He prayed she did not remain upstairs. More so, hoped that if she appeared, the sadness he had heard in her weeping was gone from her face. If it were not, he would take matters into his own hands, be damned everyone waiting for her. If he spied even an ounce of pain in her eyes, he would usher her back upstairs away from these vultures straight away.

"Are you quite well, Mr. Wright?" came a gentle, inquisitive voice beside him.

Startled that he had not seen nor heard Isabella approach when he religiously knew where everyone was in a room, he glanced her way, gathered himself, and nodded. "I am, thank you." He bowed at the waist. "Good eve to you, Lady Stanton."

"And to you." She curtsied, and her gaze drifted to the stairs. "Wishing you a lovely Martinmas. I take it you await Lady Somerset's much-anticipated arrival?"

"But of course." Although it took more effort than expected, he set aside his conflicted emotions and smiled as warmly as he could manage. "And a lovely Martinmas to you as well, my lady."

He thought that might be it and Isabella would be off, but instead, she lingered by his side. Despite the way her attention remained solely on the stairs awaiting Abby, she continued speaking to him softly. So softly, it was clear she did not want to be overheard.

"Take care with her heart, Mr. Wright, for I fear it more fragile than you think." She sipped her claret and smiled at him as though they discussed the lovely evening ahead. "Rather, perhaps give her the adventure she craves and leave it at that?"

Something about the way she said it gave him pause. Moreover, it told him she was more astute, and perhaps more worldly, than she let on.

"I intend to give her every adventure, and then some." He did not run from her challenge, for it was very much that. A dare that he measured up if he were not mistaken. Yet, his father's voice was still in his head, and he would not let that down even though he was beginning to suspect he should. "As to her heart, I cannot say." He hesitated, thinking about it but could only be blunt and say things as he saw them. Say them as he felt them when it came to Abby. "Her mind, however, intrigues me a great deal."

"Does it?" Isabella's eyebrows swept up. "And why is that?"

"Need I tell you?" He arched his brows as well. "When you are an old friend of hers, yes? Therefore, you know there is more to her than meets the eye. That an adventuresome, bright spirit like hers is not the result of an unfortunate marriage but exists in spite of it." Longing to see Abby again and make sure she was all right, he looked to the stairs. "Would I be wrong in assuming there is a part of her eager to see new things beyond England and Scotland's borders? To sample everything this world has to offer if given half a chance?"

"You would not be wrong." Isabella hesitated a moment. "All the wonders beyond our borders would suit her well, but I must once more reiterate, Mr. Wright. Take care of what lies within these borders if you ever hope to show her how broad life can really be. Otherwise, she might seem open and vivacious yet remain stuck on that balcony forever."

Unsure what to say to that, he glanced her way only to find Isabella melting into the crowd. He meant to pursue her and ask her to elaborate, but his attention was caught by Blake announcing Abby. She came downstairs on Maude's arm. He searched her face for signs of distress but found none. There were no tear-stained cheeks nor red-rimmed eyes.

If anything, she was more stunning than ever as she smiled at everyone.

So stunning in a vibrant blue gown and full of personality that, despite the cautious untrusting businessman in him, his worries faded in the shade of her radiance. The orchestra was in full swing now, and too many suitors to count were ready to lead her to the dance floor when she reached the bottom. So many that he was shocked to discover he hoped one might convince her when it had been his intention to claim that moment for himself upstairs.

To claim it so no one owned it but him.

Yet though he wanted to see her happy, he knew better than to think it would be in the arms of this parade of thieves. This house of fools with but one objective. Yes, some might argue their intentions were no different than his, but he knew better. Not one of them would offer her what she wanted most. *Needed* most.

And that was freedom.

Chapter Seven

"ARE YOU SURE you are all right?" Maude asked Abby for the umpteenth time as they walked down the stairs. "Because you need not suffer a ball if it is too much."

It was, but Abby would not disappoint her sister by dwelling on the past in her room all night. Worse yet, on a balcony that had started to feel a little less like freedom lately. Rather, it seemed a mix of old memories determined to hold her prisoner in a melancholy that had for too long become second nature behind closed doors.

A sadness she did well to overcome around others.

"I am fine." She tried not to cringe at the sea of faces below. Men who were eager to flirt and dance with her. "Though I do hope you understand that no matter how sweet your intentions with this ball, I will not be dancing."

"I am not sure what you mean by my intentions, but—"

"Of course you do." She smiled at those below as they descended. "I have heard the term 'second-chance ball' used, and I see how many men my age are here."

"Total coincidence," Maude assured.

"It is not, and you know it." When her sister went to argue again, she made things clear. "Best you admit it now. so I do not grow upset again. Because the good Lord knows, thinking my sister lied to me would be sad indeed."

Maude hesitated before she sighed. "Can you blame me for wanting to see you happy? And what better way to do that than by giving you a chance to start over? To experience something you never have before?"

"And you thought that would happen at a ball of all things?" She smiled pleasantly at her sister as if they were having a livelier conversation. "A ball where men will expect to dance with me when I do not dance anymore?"

"But I thought perhaps now—"

"You thought wrong." They had nearly reached the bottom. "So, while I'm thankful you had my best interests at heart, I fear you shall not see what you were hoping for tonight, sister."

"Yet I shall see *something* tonight, will I not?" Maude eyed her curiously. "Blake requested I gather up Isabella and meet you in the study before we became too immersed in the festivities. Do you have any idea what that might be about?"

"I do not."

Maude had no chance to respond before they reached the bottom, and Abby was surrounded by men who were, indeed, eager to dance with her. It seemed she would be saved, though.

That is, if one wanted to call it that.

"There you are, Lady Somerset." Laurence shouldered past her admirers, bowed at the waist, then held out his elbow. "I have come to escort you to Blake's study."

Oh, no. What was he up to now?

Enemy or not, she slipped her arm into his, grateful for the escape. Once free of the crowd, she frowned. "What is this about?"

"You shall see soon enough." He noted her frown. "Until then, you might look a tad more grateful that I freed you from disappointing so many suitors by not dancing with them."

"Despite making it clear to you that I very much might have," she countered. "I fear you may have overestimated how much influence your proposal has over me."

"Not at all," he said. "Though it is a proposal I would like to solidify."

"You actually did it," she exclaimed when she realized he was leading her toward Blake's study. "You wrote up a contract."

"Of course I did." Amusement lit his eyes. "I am rather shocked you did not think I would."

"Shocked when I am doubtful you are always honest in your business dealings?"

"Then might I prove you wrong." He looked at her most intently. "Only because I find myself very much wanting to start anew with you, Abby."

Anew with her? Whatever did that mean? It sounded unnerving. Especially when he said it with such determination.

"Please." Blake welcomed them inside when they arrived at the study. "Sit and enjoy a drink while we await the others." He handed her a sheet of paper as she joined Joseph, who sat in a chair near the fire. "As we are two of your witnesses, Laurence provided this earlier for Joseph and me to read over." He looked between her and Laurence. "I must admit, I find this quite unusual."

Rather than respond, Laurence looked at her most gravely before she began reading, surprising her with his transparency. "I lied to you, my dear, and I apologize. I *can*, in fact, waltz." He gestured at the paper. "That being said, please review the adjustments to our previous arrangement. A proposal I wished to have overseen by two witnesses each, so you understand just how much I mean to honor it."

She *knew* that the whole business about him not being able to waltz was a lie. A smoothly said one, at that, backing up what she had accused him of mere minutes ago. So why change his mind? Why be honest now? It was something she would be sure to follow up on.

When she'd agreed to a contract, she had not taken into consideration what that might mean. Specifically, that it would include so many people. So she was admittedly embarrassed, and more than a little worried Maude and Blake would want to further understand what this was about.

Nonetheless, Laurence had taken it this far, so she best read it over and hopefully get this done straight away. To that end, she read the document, which was very official, and the only thing that had changed was the waltz. She would not need to teach him, but she would owe him one dance whenever it suited her, as long as it happened before she danced with anyone else.

She frowned at him. "You go too far."

"It need not be in the ballroom when the time comes," he clarified. "But it needs to be mine before any others and for an entire song at that." He shrugged. "We can even pretend you are teaching me, if that is preferable."

"Oh, how very curious," Maude said as she and Isabella joined them and curtsied to Joseph. "Whatever brings us all together like this?"

Blake gestured at Abby and Laurence and explained what was happening.

"Oh, my." Maude looked over the contract before she grew amused and surprised them all when she looked at Laurence. "Does this have anything to do with you blackmailing my sister because she presented herself as a common trollop when you first met?"

When Abby narrowed her eyes at Isabella, her friend offered a weak little shrug. "You know I cannot keep secrets from Maude, dear friend." Equal amusement flashed in her eyes when she gestured Maude's way. "She has a way of seeing right through me and Margaret."

"No doubt," Abby muttered. They clearly found this quite the game. She perked a brow at Blake. "Should I assume you know all the sordid details as well?"

"I am afraid so." He shot Laurence a grim look as he handed out cocktails. "And while understandable you wanted a bit of an escape, such as it were, Abby, I cannot say I much approve of Laurence's proposal to you. Better still, the threat behind it."

"Nor I," Joseph concurred, plainly knowing all the details as well. "Blackmail is not recommended in any circumstance, let alone when trying to secure a wife."

"Yet it certainly speaks to his determination," Maude mused, not as put off as she should be. "And his requests are not all that bad."

"No, they are not." Laurence shocked Abby when he pulled out a second contract and looked at her. "Yet my friends are right. I should have never blackmailed you, Abby." He handed it to her. "So, I would like to revise my proposal so that it only encompasses me no longer pursuing you and leaving you in peace after you see through my stipulations." He shook his head. "There will be no further talk of tavern behavior. Contract or not, that threat is entirely extinguished."

"That is *much* better indeed." Maude clasped her hands together in delight and grinned at Laurence. "Well done!"

"Maude," she exclaimed, frowning at her sister. "He is *still* holding something over me."

"Yes, but it is the threat of mere courtship, dear sister," Maude pointed out. "Something I imagine you are going to deal with quite often with men, so why not enjoy such a generous offer attached to it?" She arched her eyebrows at Laurence. "As I suspect, Mr. Wright intends to pay for everything?"

"I do." He smiled at Abby with reassurance. "You will not have to spend a shilling, love."

"Lady Somerset."

"Abby?"

"No."

"My lady?"

"No."

He smirked. "Then, my little trollop?"

She rounded her eyes. "Goodness, *no*." Then she frowned. "Fine. Abigail."

"I prefer Abby."

"Yet that is reserved for friends, and you are no such thing."

"Then I shall make it my mission to become such."

"Good luck."

"Now, that is something I tend to possess." Laurence gestured at the new contract. "So, what say you, Abigail? Will you sign our contract in exchange for one less nuisance? Because rest assured, I am relentless when it comes to something I want, and I cannot imagine you desire to deal with that the rest of your life." He gestured at Blake and Joseph. "Just ask them how driven I can be."

"Relentless indeed," Joseph confirmed. "So, given the contract's adjustment, I cannot help but recommend that you sign it." He wore a small, bemused smile when he glanced from Laurence to her. "Either you will be rid of my friend's relentless pursuit, or you will perhaps end up revising your opinion about him."

"That will not happen." She reminded Laurence, most of all, where she stood. "As I will *not* marry again."

"I understand." His gaze seemed to dare her. "Are you ready to sign it? Or shall I plan on pursuing you so avidly that I drive you mad?"

While she would have liked to remind Maude and Isabella that he was trying to imprison her as much as Reginald had, she knew they would not see it that way. Not when he'd managed to address their two biggest concerns when it came to her. Dancing and traveling. Both were much overdue indulgences, in their opinions. She looked from Isabella to Maude in question, only for them to shrug and smile, which told her they would be of no help.

This decision was hers.

While it seemed a rather simple one, it was anything but. She would have a formidable opponent in Laurence because, she suspected, he would make the best use of his time with her. He would no longer sit back and watch but become an active participant in pursuing her. Given his recent honesty, she feared that pursuit being less off-putting than before, too. Rather, she got the sense he was switching tactics altogether and coming at her from a whole new direction.

She was not sure which way that was yet, but it had her more on guard than ever.

Even so, this would at least curb the amount of time she had to fend him off. Perhaps cut down the risk of her heart falling victim where it should not. With that in mind, she looked at him and nodded. "All right, I will sign it."

His grin widened into such a genuinely happy smile that her heart did a little unexpected leap. One she did not much trust as everyone proceeded to sign the contract. After signing the last signature, Maude beamed at Abby and Laurence and raised her glass in a toast.

"Here is to waltzing and traveling," she said. "May you enjoy doing both together."

Even though Abby did not raise her glass and drink alongside the others, she did feel a surge of excitement that she would finally step foot on a boat. She could only hope she didn't have to dodge Laurence's advances at every turn, as she could not imagine them enjoying a civil conversation. Nor could she see them having anything in common.

"I must say you surprised me back there with both your honesty and change of stipulations," she said when it became clear after they left Blake's study that he would remain by her side. "Whatever possessed you?"

"Why, *you*, Abigail." He appeared a well-contented kitten. Better yet, a well-satisfied tiger that had caught its prey. "I find I would much rather have your affection than your dislike."

She rolled her eyes. "Whatever would you want that for?"

"I could not say entirely as I have never felt this way before." Laurence sipped his whisky and spoke casually despite admitting something rather profound. "All I know is I desire more than wedding and bedding you now." He tilted his head and thought about it. "I want to understand you better. What makes you happy, sad, and joyous."

"So that you might somehow use it to get your way?"

"In part, I imagine so," he admitted, blunt as ever, yet perplexed as well when his blue-eyed gaze lingered on her. A lock of blond hair fell over his forehead, and the corners of his mouth curved up ever so slightly. His gaze lingered on her. "But that is not the sole reason."

A little breathless at the way he looked at her, she frowned back at him in equal confusion. "Then what is?"

"I cannot quite say," he said softly, as though whatever it was possessed the ability to humble him. "Only that it's a driving force that cannot be ignored."

She did her best not to warm at the intensity in his eyes and the passion in his voice. "Yet I suspect you must."

"Why?"

She had no chance to respond before a notable and much-beloved duke and duchess were announced at the door.

"Dear sister, I did not know you were coming tonight!" Caring not for decorum, Abby closed the distance between her and Prudence and embraced her. "Oh, how I have missed you."

"And I have missed you." Prudence hugged her tightly, then held her at arm's length and looked her over with approval. "How very stunning you look."

"And you, as always." She smiled and curtsied to Prudence's husband, Jacob. "So very good to see you again, brother." It was impossible not to see how much he and her sister loved one another. "Did you bring my precious nephew with you?"

"Not this visit, as we are traveling a tad too much." Prudence squeezed her hand. "I do so hope you will visit Charles and Grace with us after our visit here. I am so eager to meet our new niece and see our nephew again."

Very much looking forward to it, she smiled. "Absolutely, I shall join you."

"And this is?" Prudence prompted, only for Abby to realize Laurence had remained by her side.

"This would be Mr. Wright. Blake and Maude's guest from America." She gestured at her kin. "Mr. Wright, may I introduce the Duke and Duchess of Argyll."

"How delightful." As her station was too high to curtsy, Prudence smiled warmly. "All the way from America, then? I do hope you have enjoyed our country so far."

"Thank you, Your Grace." Laurence's telling gaze lingered on Abby for a moment before he returned Prudence's smile and bowed. "Very much so, at that."

"I see." Her sister's perceptive gaze went from Abby to him, and her smile grew warmer still. "I look forward to speaking with you, Mr. Wright, for it is far too rare that we enjoy American guests."

"As do I, you, Your Grace."

"By God, are you Blake's longtime American friend from Boston?" Jacob exclaimed, his Scottish brogue a tad thicker than usual. "The infamous heir to the Wright fortune?"

"Indeed." Laurence grinned. "And you are Jacob, his dearest childhood friend, yes?"

"Aye, one of them anyway." Throwing decorum to the wind every bit as much as Abby had, he shook Laurence's hand and met his grin. "Such a pleasure to meet you, Laurence. I have heard only good things." Clearly impressed, Jacob's smile only widened. "You shall have to meet Blake's other childhood friend, Charles, while you are here. He has embarked on several business ventures lately that might be of interest to you."

"Such as?"

"Shipbuilding, for starters," Jacob divulged. "He has figured out a way to build them faster than most and intends to capitalize on that."

"How much faster?"

"Nearly twice as fast as they could in the past."

"Does quality suffer?"

"No." Jacob shook his head. "If anything, they are better made than most."

"Twice as fast?" Laurence's eyebrows shot up. "As well as superior quality?"

"Indeed."

"Tell me more."

"And that, dear gentlemen—" Prudence linked arms with Abby—"is where we ladies shove off to enjoy the festivities."

Grateful for the escape from Laurence, Abby strolled away from talk of business despite how much it had intrigued her. She found how well Laurence and Jacob got along mildly unsettling. Not in a bad way, either, but in a fashion that seemed to unlock muscles in her shoulders she'd not realized had grown so tense.

"My, *my*, sister, look who you attracted in so little time?" Prudence praised the moment they were out of earshot. "I have never seen a man look at you like that before. And an American, no less. What a divine turn of events." She grinned. "I always knew you were meant for splendid things, but never imagined it would be someone who suited your adventuresome spirit so well."

She was not sure where to begin with everything Prudence had just declared, only that she would rather do it beyond curious ears, so she steered them down a hallway containing fewer people.

"To be clear, so you have your facts up front," she said, "Laurence is absolutely not my match but a downright scoundrel." She frowned. "Just wait until you hear why."

"Oh, yes, do tell me all the horrid details." Prudence grinned and waved over a servant with a tray of cocktails. "Do not leave out a thing." She took a glass of claret and replaced Abby's with a fuller one. "Because you two have a certain *je ne sais quoi*, I do not know what, only that it is bound to set your soul afire, dear sister."

"My soul? Afire?" She liked seeing her sister so happy and carefree again, but this was a bit much. At least when it came to her and Laurence. "How very vividly poetic of you but quite wrong, I fear." She shook her head. "I am fairly certain I never disliked a man more."

"Just as I thought I did my Jacob but was never more wrong."

"We are not you and Jacob," she made clear. "Of that, you can rest assured."

"Then tell me all about it." Prudence set aside her smile and became the big sister she needed. "Tell me what I missed so I might lend you comfort or assure you that you and your American are exactly what I suspected the moment I saw you two together."

Chapter Eight

WHILE LAURENCE LOATHED the missed opportunity to talk with Abby rather than just banter, flirt, or endlessly desire her, he found his conversation with Jacob worthwhile. Not only that, but it revealed an opportunity that perhaps could become remarkably lucrative—*if* he could overcome one sizeable hurdle.

"I must admit, I'm interested in meeting Charles and perhaps going into business with him," he said to Jacob as they enjoyed a whisky together in Blake's study and got to know one another better. Something it seemed Jacob, despite being a duke, had made a priority. "But I would be remiss if I did not point out my financial aid might not be well received considering his history."

"A valid concern," Jacob conceded. "While Charles lost a great deal fighting the Americans during the war, I have never heard him speak ill of your countrymen when at his best."

He arched an eyebrow. "So, should I assume he has when at his worst?"

Jacob explained how Charles sometimes suffered from a post-war affliction of the mind. He experienced moments of melancholy and rage where on occasion, he railed against Laurence's countrymen.

"I tell you this in the vein of honesty so you might have all your facts upfront if you decide to go into business with him," Jacob said. "That said, he has much improved since falling in love with Grace." Clearly glad to have his friend returned to him, he seemed to gather himself a moment before continuing. "Such a marked difference—a healing if you will—that I can say with utmost confidence he would be a worthy business partner." He shook his head. "He would not let you down."

"On that, we certainly agree," Blake said from the door, grinning at Jacob. "Welcome back, old chap. Apologies that I missed your arrival." He poured himself a whisky, sat as well, and nodded once at Laurence. "Meet Charles, and you will see we are right. Moreover, I imagine you will be most impressed."

Even though he did not trust someone improved merely by love alone, he could admit Jacob had spun quite the tale of a changed man. One who had a very good head for business.

"As you know, while I did not claim to be singularly federalist at the time, I did not support the War of 1812," he said. "Will that matter to Charles, or is it a moot point?"

"It's impossible to know as, outside of his internal battles, he rarely speaks of his time in the Royal Navy," Jacob said. "Either good or bad."

Where typically, he would say no to this for the mental instability angle of things alone, Charles's business ideas were superb. Even so, there was more to consider. Something he was shocked to realize meant more than the idea of expanding his empire.

"What will happen if I meet him and decide not to go into business?" He looked from Jacob to Blake. "How would Abby take it? Because I will not risk upsetting her if I decline. Having her in my life is far too important to chance losing her over a business deal." He cleared his throat and clarified. "What I mean to say is having her as my wife is too important."

When Jacob seemed unsure what that meant, Blake caught him up on everything he had missed. Where he thought the duke would be appalled, Jacob chuckled instead. "And here I thought we Scots were crazy when it came to love." He shook his head. "Yet it seems you Americans might have us beat." His chuckle turned to outright laughter. "You swindled Abby into doing the two things she needed most in life? Became the unknown savior she does not see coming, for the sake of love? Bloody brilliant!"

"I assure you love is not part of this." He frowned at Blake, who only looked amused and shrugged. "This is a business arrangement, nothing more."

"Of course, it is, friend." Jacob's laughter ceased but not his smile. "Perhaps it would be better if Blake or I send a letter ahead about your impending arrival and see how Charles responds. That way, you are not walking into a wasp's nest and risking Abby's love." He cleared his throat as well. "I mean, risking anything that keeps her from seeing through the business arrangement of your marriage."

Although he did not know Jacob nearly enough to be amused, he knew better than to respond with anything but professionalism. "I think that would be wise." Essential, really. "Thank you."

While they went on to talk for a bit after that, nothing more was said about Charles or Abby. She was never far from his mind, though. What was she doing at this very moment? Flirting with another? Enchanting too many men to count? Turning down dance upon dance because she was obligated to him?

She best be, or else.

He flinched at the thought because it reminded him too much of how his father had spoken to his mother. No doubt the reason she turned from them in the end. His father, because of his controlling nature, and, in turn, Laurence, because he was underneath his father's thumb. When that happened, his father had grown especially ruthless. He cut his losses and moved on, grooming his son in his image. He might have failed at marriage but would not fail at the cold-hearted business of ensuring Laurence was worthy of his inheritance.

In no mood to let his father influence his thoughts, he downed the last of his whisky and scanned the great hall for Abby after leaving the study. When he did not see her, he made his way into the ballroom, but she was not there, either.

"If you are looking for my sister, Abby, I am afraid you will not find her here, Mr. Wright," Prudence said, joining him. She watched the twirling couples on the dance floor for a moment before her gaze drifted his way. "Then again, why would you when she is beholden to a contract that disallows her from dancing with another?"

"And what are your thoughts on that, my lady?" He wondered how much influence she might have had over Abby in the brief time she'd been here and especially what other hurdles he might have to leap now.

"I find it arrogant, presumptuous, outrageous, and more than a tad over the top." The corner of her mouth curled up. "Yet, it's precisely what my sister needs." Before he could reply, she narrowed her eyes. "That said, do not mistake my approval for a lack of concern nor support of you if you harm her heart in any way. Do that, and I will personally see you on the first ship back to America, may your money never touch our shores again. Furthermore, I will ensure your good name is ruined in these parts, and do not for a moment think I lack the means to do it, Mr. Wright."

Yet again, Abby's vulnerable heart was mentioned when it came to him. Had anyone actually talked to her? Understood he would be the last person in whom she would invest her heart?

"Laurence," he corrected. Where some might be offended, he had suffered more than his fair share of threats over the years. "As to harming Abby's heart, rest assured, that is the very last thing I wish to do." Yet his curiosity was piqued, so he fished. "But then, you understand her heart is very much closed off to me, yes?"

Prudence frowned and eyed him for a moment in a way he could not quite understand before she seemed to see something in him, and her brows flew up. "Good Lord, you are as bad off as her, are you not, Mr. Wright? You are just as ignorant despite your vast intelligence?"

"Please call me Laurence." He frowned and shook his head. "And I do not follow your meaning, Your Grace."

"Hence your ignorance when it comes to matters of the heart." She held out her elbow. "Stroll with me, Mr. Wright, so I might give you a much-needed lesson in love. One I had nearly forgotten myself until Jacob came back into my life."

More intrigued by the moment, he slipped his arm into hers, and they strolled out of the ballroom into a quieter corridor.

"Much like you—" Prudence began before she shook her head—"no, *exactly* like you, Abby knows nothing of true love. She can romanticize about what it might feel like but has never experienced it, so she has nothing to fall back on. No real experience to validate her claim that she understands what love is—or is not."

She considered him for a moment as if debating just how much to say before continuing.

"At one time, in our youth, Abby was even more of a romantic than I." Her smile grew whimsical. "She was so full of life and hope. Utterly naïve but wonderfully charming. She saw the world through a spectrum of timeless love and grand adventures. Of stolen, passionate kisses and a doting husband who would grant her every wish. Who would sweep her off her feet and give her the world." She gave him a pointed look. "Most of all, though, he would give her his heart. Love her as fiercely as she loved him."

"That must have been something," he said softly, wishing he could peer through time and see that young girl. Even so, had it all been truly lost? He was not so certain and said so. "Yet it is not lost." He shook his head, seeing that same radiance in Abby now. "Not all of that wonder has been vanquished. Surely you can see it as clearly as I?"

"I can." Yet she did not seem all that happy about it. "But I suspect it a front more often than not. A front I was never able to achieve in my last marriage." She sighed. "Rather, I gave into bitterness and resentment rather than push past it when I needed to for the sake of others." Prudence seemed somewhere else for a moment before narrowing in on him again. "My sister is far stronger than I am, and I fear it cost her something she is only now realizing." She stopped walking and tilted her head at him. "Much like you might be, realizing the same of your circumstances, Mr. Wright?"

"I'm sure I do not know what you mean." *Or did he?*

"I imagine you do not, but soon will if you are even half as intelligent as I suspect." She kept looking at him in a rather all-knowing fashion. "While you are clearly smitten with Abby's appearance and, no doubt, her beguiling, vivacious spirit, have you taken the time to get to know her yet? To really talk to her?"

"Not as much as I would have liked."

"And is that your fault or hers?"

"Mine," he confessed without a second thought because it *had* been from the moment he'd thought her a trollop to deciding she would be his wife.

"Why?"

"Because that is how I do business," he said frankly, starting to see the error of his ways. "I assess a deal, weigh the probability of success, and move forward if I think it's worth it."

"So, Abby became an opportunity rather than a woman?"

"Oh, she might have been a goal but was always a woman." Of that, there could be no doubt. Yet he saw her point. One he could have cared less about weeks before. "Very much a woman and more so by the day."

A small smile curled Prudence's mouth as she considered him. "I dare say, how does one become *more* of a woman?"

He shook his head because he had no logical answer.

"I think perhaps you should finally stop merely ogling my sister and take the time to speak with her, Laurence," Prudence said. "Take the time to understand why you cannot answer the question I just asked you."

Quite liking this sister, he met her small smile. "Why not just tell me since matters of the heart seem very much a business you excel at?"

A telling sparkle lit her eyes. "I won't because half the magic is in figuring it out for yourself." She leaned in a tad closer. A means to be discreet, as it happened. "Until then, without a doubt, eager to have her previous adventuresome spirit resurrected, you might find Abby lingering around that vine."

He frowned in confusion before he realized what she meant and shook his head in alarm. "Surely *not*."

There was no way she would actually try to climb it, was there? He could only pray not.

Rather than wait for a response, he flew down the corridor and out the door, then raced around the castle, only to slow when he heard weeping again. This time not from above but coming from beneath Abby's balcony. Panicked that she had attempted to climb the damn vine and hurt herself, he ran over only to find her not broken on the ground but leaning back against the castle, gripping the vine beside her.

"Abby, are you all right?" Frightened in a way that was foreign to him, he looked her up and down, searching for any sign of injury, then spoke more harshly than intended when she did not respond right away. "Are you well, Abby?" He cupped her shoulder and the side of her waist lest she was trying to hold herself up. "*Say* something. Tell me now."

When he went to scoop her up upon receiving no immediate response, she whispered hoarsely, "I am fine. Just give me a moment."

Fortunately, torches had been lit along this walkway for the holiday, so he was able to see her clearly. See her nod of reassurance and the truth of it in her eyes.

"You should sit." He gestured behind him. "There is a bench right there, so sit and rest. Gather yourself." When she did not respond right away, he became more insistent. "Come sit, Abby. Please."

"I do not want to sit," she said in a strained whisper before clearing her voice. "I feel like I have been sitting my whole blasted life."

Surprised by her sudden vehemence, he nodded slowly, understanding just how upset she was. "Then we will stand." He gently wiped away a tear on one soft cheek. "We will do whatever you wish." Pained for her, he wiped a tear from the other cheek. "We will stand as long as you like."

She eyed him warily for several moments before she murmured, "Why are you being so kind?"

Why did she seem so baffled by that? "Am I not always kind?"

"Are you *serious?*" She released a little burst of strained, choppy laughter before she grew quite somber. "No, Laurence, you are not always kind. Rather, one way or another, you have been an unfeeling monster since the moment we reconnected here at MacLauchlin Castle."

Having never heard himself described that way by a woman, he frowned. "That is rather harsh, is it not?"

"No," Abby exclaimed, shaking the vine still in her hand. "Since the moment you climbed this and started blackmailing me, you have been atrocious." She scowled, quite heated now. "Every bit as awful as my late husband was at the beginning."

So it was true. She had not always thought poorly of Reginald.

While typically, he would counter that with something positive he had done, namely his wish to offer her an extraordinarily lucrative future, he could not seem to say it. Not when he saw the pain in her gaze. An inner torture that spoke to him on a level he did not understand.

And he feared it.

Feared how quickly it could take her away from him.

"You are right." He removed his tailcoat, wrapped it around her shoulders, cupped the side of her neck, and nodded. "I have been awful, and I'm sorry, Abigail. Truly very sorry."

As if uncertain she had heard him correctly, she blinked a few times and shook her head. "No," she whispered, as if seeing something in his gaze she did not trust. "You cannot be. Would not know *how* to be."

"Yet I am." Rather than give into the desire touching her invoked, he pulled away and nodded. "More than you can possibly imagine."

"Why?"

"I don't know." He glanced from the vine to her. "All I know is the thought of you climbing that and harming yourself did not sit well. Nor did lying to you about being able to waltz." He raked a hand through his hair. "Or, ultimately, the blackmail that led to our contract."

Abby frowned. "How can you not know?" She shook her head. "Because I find that answer most unacceptable."

"Yet it is one that eludes even me." He sighed and leaned against the wall beside her when he only wanted to pull her into his arms and hold her. Defying emotions he could not control, he crossed his arms over his chest. "All I know is despite having known you for such a short time, there is something about you I find most—" he struggled for the right word but could only think of one—"kindred."

"You are playing again." She sounded incredulous. "You are feeding off whatever you might have learned about me to accomplish your goals."

"I would like to think so as that would feel decidedly better than whatever this is," he admitted. "Feel more like myself." He frowned at her. "Yet I am being honest. Painfully so, at that."

Abby seemed as baffled as he felt as she eyed him. "You actually are, I think."

"Good, because I am." Wanting the truth from her just as much, he cocked his head. "What happened, Abigail? Why are you out here? Why were you gripping that vine and weeping on a cold, windy night?"

"Because I wanted…"

When she trailed off and shook her head, he urged her to go on. "Wanted what?"

He would give her the world if she only asked for it.

"I do not know," she said.

"Yes, you do."

"Not really."

"Just tell me." He wrapped his fingers with hers before he could stop himself. Held a woman's hand for the very first time ever and looked from the vine to her. "Why, Abigail?"

"Because I wanted to know if I might have been able to manage it either way," she confessed softly. Her gaze drifted up the length of the vine. "I wanted to know if I might have escaped three years ago. That first visit here when Reginald was so…"

"What?" he prompted gently after giving her a moment to gather herself.

"So very disagreeable not just to staff but people in general," she said. "He was not pleasant as a rule but pompous and cruel."

"And to you?" he assumed.

"Not so much to me." She shook her head. "He certainly got in bad moods, but mostly he completely ignored me when we were alone. I was simply a means to satisfy how he wanted others to perceive him. Nothing more than a prop in a marriage of convenience."

He was not sure what caught him more unaware. That Reginald was never abusive or cruel to her or that there was a daunting parallel to be drawn between him and her late husband.

"Why now, though?" He glanced at the vine, unsure he wanted to hear the answer. "Why are you so eager to see if you can escape when it no longer matters?"

"Because, for some reason, it still does."

"Might that reason be me?" he wondered, seeing it clearly enough.

"Perhaps," she murmured. "I cannot say for certain as this is my first visit back to MacLauchlin Castle since Reginald passed, so it could very well be a latent longing, so to speak."

"One I fed right into when I climbed this vine."

He was baffled by how much he had mistakenly become part of something that had been all hers. A terrible longing that was a testament to the freedom she had craved. A freedom and vine of hope that he, oddly enough, understood. One he could empathize with more than she could imagine.

That said, he knew there was only one way this night could end.

The way something inside him demanded it to end, no matter how much he'd hoped it would be with her in his arms.

Chapter Nine

AFTER ABBY TOLD Prudence everything about Laurence and how she had ended up signing a preposterous contract born of first blackmail, then a wicked ultimatum, she'd waited for her sister's wrath. Knew she would be appalled for sure.

But, alas, she had not been.

Instead, Prudence had seemed quite matter of fact and irritatingly businesslike, yet somehow still atrociously amused. "So let me get this straight, little sister." She'd narrowed her eyes and tapped a fingernail against her glass. "You decided to dress and act like a commoner for a night of fun in a busy tavern and bumped into a handsome foreigner who you decided should think you a trollop to lend a tad more excitement to the whole thing?" Her brows had shot up. "Yet, the moment you realized he was traveling here, you confessed you were no trollop and fled from him."

Prudence had chuckled and carried on.

"Then, once you arrived here, despite undoubtedly stealing your American's heart in such a brief and scandalous encounter, you discovered who he was and vice versa." She'd chuckled again. "And then, lo and behold, and quite frankly, not surprisingly enough, the two of you found your way to a signed contract of all things that would keep you locked together until you share one entire dance and one trip in a boat." She had cocked her head. "Worded just like that in said contract? One you signed with multiple witnesses?"

"Yes," she'd said tentatively, not sure where her sister was going with this. "Why do you sound so irritatingly amused?"

"Because you have a wonderfully trusting heart that I do so adore. Now, you also possess a rabid need to break free from this man for the threat he presents to said heart." Prudence had squeezed her hand and looked at her ruefully. "Darling, the contract says one full dance, so I imagine Mr. Wright will find a way to cease many dances before the song is over. That keeps you in his arms far longer. As we are heading into winter, and it is no time for a woman to sail anywhere far, I suspect you will not travel until spring." The corner of her mouth had curled up. "That gives our clever American more time still. Quite a bit of it, actually."

While she had not paid attention to wording when it came to their waltz, she had realized what the traveling aspect of it entailed. "He intends to be here for months on business, so nothing is astray, sister." She'd shrugged. "As to dancing, let him try to stop before I get my song and end it accordingly."

"Yes, of course." Prudence had looked at her with reassurance. "I apologize for thinking you did not have this all under control. That was rather uncalled for, yes?"

Where some might get aggravated, she knew better. Her sisters only ever looked out for her, just like she did them. "It *was* called for, and you know it." She sighed. "You are right, and I wish I could tell you why I still agreed to the contract, but I have no answer." *Why was that? What was the matter with her?* "No reason other than an overwhelming need to escape."

"And that is the very best reason." Without a doubt, reflecting on her own past, Prudence had seemed a tad sad when she'd squeezed Abby's hand again. "Just remember from whom you are trying to escape, sister, because I fear you might not be focused on the correct villain."

"Reginald was not a villain," she'd said, a bit too intensely, but she'd meant it. "Not to me. *Never* to me."

"All right," Prudence had said gently. Carefully. "Even so." Well aware that she'd intended to step outside to clear her head, her sister had cupped Abby's cheek. "When you go outside and visit your balcony from below, because I am quite sure that is where you are headed, focus on letting the past go so you might see the present more clearly."

No less confused than she'd been inside, she now gripped the vine beneath her balcony with Laurence by her side. More confusing still, her villain seemed less and less villainous by the moment. Or so he appeared when really, it could just be that he'd caught her in such a vulnerable moment.

She had been so close to climbing the vine, her inappropriate clothing be damned but then she'd turned coward. So close to seeing if she could manage it or if it had always been a foolish fantasy. A ridiculous one at that, as there was no escaping marriage. And in those last few years, she would have never forgiven herself had she somehow been able to.

"I'm sorry for climbing the vine if it caused you that kind of pain, Abigail," Laurence said softly, pulling her back to the present and his surprisingly supportive presence. To how his warm hand felt in hers. "I will not do that again."

Where she thought for sure he would try to seduce her, he did the very opposite.

"Come." He pushed away from the wall. "I know another way to your chamber other than this vine that avoids the crowd inside. This night might be for you, but perhaps it is better met alone and resting?"

Assuming he meant with him, she shook her head. "I will not be lying with you."

"Nor did I expect it of you." He tugged at her hand a little. "I realize you have no reason to trust me, but allow me to escort you to your room, Abigail. Trust that I will attempt nothing along the way."

Recalling how fearful and then tender he had been when he'd

come across her weeping of all things, she could not help but give in and let him lead her away from the vine. Away from a balcony, she was determined to conquer in a way she did not fully understand.

"I should go back to the ball," she said. "While yes, it is a holiday, Maude and Blake went above and beyond for me. To go to sleep would be rude even though, truth told, it is all I long for right now."

"And I imagine something Maude would insist upon if she knew you needed it." He never let go of her hand as he led her up a dark, twisting stairwell. A secluded place he would have most certainly taken advantage of days before.

Not now, though, as he miraculously escorted her to her door just as promised without expecting a thing in return. Rather, he looked at her with touching concern. "Will you be all right, Abigail?"

"I think so," she whispered when she could not find her voice. "Hope so."

"You will." He leaned in and kissed her cheek. A brief, gentle kiss that, while certainly making her aware of him, was not untoward or sensual. Instead, when his gaze found her face again, she was rather taken aback by how much he seemed to care. "Rest well, Lady Abigail. I will see Miss Eleanor sent up and will not be far if you need me."

Then, just like that, he vanished downstairs, and she was alone.

While abrupt, it somehow suited him. He had melted out of the night like a dashing hero and then vanished so quickly that he might have been a dream. Might have been the sort she envisioned years ago when she imagined the man who would sweep her into his arms at her coming-out ball. The handsome stranger who made her feel all sorts of delicious things and kissed her so passionately, the world faded away.

She knew better than to think that could ever be Laurence, but he certainly would have been her dream husband had he been less selfish. As to his behavior now, she suspected it was temporary. A means to an end because the real man could not meet the criteria of a dashing hero.

Or so she thought until Eleanor woke her the next morning.

"My lady," she said softly but urgently as she shook Abby out of a rather deep slumber. "You must wake up straight away."

"What is it?" She yawned and tried to make sense of what was going on. From what she could tell, the sun had barely crested the horizon.

"It is him, my lady." Eleanor kept shaking her. "You must wake, for I do not know what to do. If I tell anyone else, your good name could be ruined."

She blinked and sat up, more confused than ever. "Why?"

"You shall soon see." Desperate and wide-eyed, Eleanor pulled at her wrist, then wrapped a coat around her shoulders the moment she stood. "Please, my lady, straight away!"

Stumbling after her maid to the door to the balcony, she frowned. "What is it, Eleanor? What is so dire that you need…"

She trailed off when Eleanor put a finger to her lips and pointed at something just beyond the door. Both tentative and concerned, Abby opened it and peeked out only to find Laurence sound asleep in the chair closest to the vine. Her maid kept a finger to her mouth and pointed over the edge of the balcony.

Abby's mouth dropped when she peered down, only to discover a ladder that reached her balcony. What had the fool been up to last night other than trying to freeze to death? Baffled, she looked from the ladder to Laurence, whose breath hit the cold air in steamy puffs.

"Inside, Eleanor," she mouthed, ushering her maid back inside, where she gave Eleanor a most dire look. "How much do we trust Mr. Wright's valet?"

"I know not." Eleanor's eyes grew rather dreamy. "Though he is quite handsome in his own way."

God help her. "Is he to be trusted, Eleanor?"

"I could not say." She tilted her head and thought about it.

"Though perhaps he *can* be, considering Harold has been asking questions about you and your late husband below stairs. Many suspect it is so his master can learn more about you, but his valet denies it."

So *that* was how he was finding out intimate details about her.

"Can I trust you to be discreet, my friend?" She was sure to keep her expression most serious. "Trust you above all?"

"You most certainly can, my lady." Eleanor's eyes went wide, and she nodded. "Always, for I would do anything for you. Anything you need, no matter—"

"Good." She nudged Eleanor toward the door. "Then there is no time to waste. Wake Harold and have him help you bring up wood, food, and a warm change of clothing for Mr. Wright."

She might have been raised by a baron, but she'd also been raised by a commoner mother, and Maude, her wonderfully common sister, who had taught her the basic survival behaviors most of Abby's society, whose needs were supplied by servants, would not know. To that end, she stacked the remaining few pieces of wood strategically on her dying fire so they would catch well. Then, she dragged a chair close to the flames and headed back onto the balcony. Not wasting time when it had been dangerous for him to sleep out here in the first place, she shook Laurence's shoulder, only for him to lift his head in alarm.

"You fool." She took his icy hand when he looked at her in confusion before seeming a tad guilty. "Come inside before someone sees you."

"I meant no harm," he said hoarsely, his voice clearly off from breathing in the cold, damp air all night. "I was just..." He yawned and managed a small, utterly charming smile despite his foolishness. "Trying to protect you."

"Protect me from whom?" She frowned and made him sit in front of the fire. "I am perfectly safe."

"Are you, though, my lady?" He visibly shivered now. "Because I'm not so sure."

"So, you climbed a ladder onto my balcony?" She yanked a blanket off her bed and wrapped it around his shoulders. "Though I suppose that is safer than the vine."

"Indeed." His eyes seemed adrift when he tried to focus on her. "I feared you might try the vine again, so I built a ladder." He shrugged. "Then I feared you might try the ladder, so I stood guard."

"Come again?" She thought the ladder appeared rather new. "You built a ladder last night for me to climb down?"

"I did," he slurred and yawned again. "And I think you might find the length between steps suited to your height."

Worried because he seemed quite off, she yanked at his hand to stand again. "Come, you need to lie down, Laurence."

"With you?" His eyes were half-mast as he grinned. "I thought you would never ask."

"And I did not." Thankfully, he gave no issue but trudged after her to the bed until she could push him down, and he fell quite neatly. "Nor will I ask."

"But you should." Laurence smiled as she grunted and steered his feet until he lay down entirely. "For you will be pleasantly pleased, my love." He wagged a finger and squinted one eye at her. "No, no, not love but Mrs. Wright." His smile only grew, and he chuckled. "I mean 'Mrs. Right,' as you are so very *right* for me."

Figuring out he was not just cold but borderline inebriated, she rolled her eyes. "So we have skipped Lady Somerset, my lady, and Abby, have we?"

"Most certainly, *my lady* but never *Abby*." He seemed to consider things as she worked at pulling off his shoes. "As to Lady Somerset, I do not think we should abandon him just yet. Not until we further understand him."

"You mean Lord Somerset."

"Indeed!"

She was not sure what to make of that other than he seemed to have gleaned more than she anticipated from last night. A great deal if that ladder were anything to go off of.

"I fear I have let you down, Lady Love," Laurence slurred as she retrieved the blanket that had fallen from his shoulders onto the floor. "I did not mean to—" he narrowed his eyes, very much having a conversation with himself—"well, I *did* mean to bed you the minute I saw you, as did every man in there." He snorted and shook his head. "But I knew when I touched you and looked into your eyes…" Another chuckle and a hearty sigh as she covered him with her blanket. "I knew you would only ever be mine. That I would make you feel things you could never have imagined, and I would start with…"

When his words turned into indiscernible mumbles, she should have steered clear, but she was too curious for her own good and wanted to hear more. Where *would* he start? What would he do? So, she leaned close and urged him on.

"Where would you start, Laurence?" she whispered, despite his eyes being closed. "What would you—"

Her words were stolen away when he suddenly cupped her cheek, and his lips grabbed hers. It was impossible to know how present he really was, but somehow it did not matter as he angled his mouth and kissed her more deeply. Kissed her as though starved for the taste of her.

In a way she had never been kissed before.

He kissed her so deeply she tasted the faint hint of whisky on his breath. The passion beyond that. A sensation so heady and intoxicating she had no choice but to kiss him back. When she did, she found the act so much better than she had imagined. In fact, it felt so good that she did not hear the knock at her door until it became more of a bang.

Jolting back, she went to see what sort of look Laurence might have in his eyes, how profoundly this moment might have touched him too, only to find his eyes closed. *He had fallen asleep!*

"I'm coming," she muttered, unsure how she should feel. Offended that he had fallen asleep almost as soon as he kissed her seemed to be at the forefront of her mind, though. *Very* much at the forefront, if she were to be honest.

Had he felt how good it had been between them? Better still, would he even remember kissing her? She likely would until her dying day. Flustered and aggravated, she opened the door, expecting to see Harold and Eleanor, only to find four brightly smiling faces.

"You cannot be *serious*," she exclaimed as Maude, Prudence, Isabella, and Margaret swept into her room still in their dressing gowns and robes. "We are not children anymore!"

"No." Isabella eyed Laurence with as much amusement and curiosity as the others. "But we are still the ones who covered for you and this dashing American last night."

"We did not do anything untoward," Abby vowed, shaking her head. "He escorted me back to my room, and that was it. He was a perfect gentleman, and I most certainly was not interested."

"Of course he did," Isabella said, drifting toward the balcony.

"And naturally, you were not interested, Abby," Margaret agreed with amusement, following Isabella.

"What are you doing?" She frowned and gestured that they leave, but instead, they all headed out onto the balcony and yanked her out after them before shutting the door.

"He really did it," Margaret exclaimed in delight, peering over the edge at the ladder. "Just look."

"My goodness, there it is." Isabella seemed just as enamored as Margaret by said ladder. "And there's a second shorter one, too, so it merely looks like construction was being done rather than someone trying to sneak up to Abby's room."

There was a second ladder? She had not noticed.

"I never doubted he would accomplish his goals." Maude grinned at Abby. "He worked on your ladder all night."

When Abby shook her head, baffled and more than a little overwhelmed by how many knew about this, Prudence rested her hand on her shoulder. "All is well, sister." She gestured at her co-conspirators. "We made sure his secret was kept safe."

"And how did you manage that?" She frowned in the direction of the ladder. "People had to have spied him carrying it here? Most certainly noticed that it was somebody other than a servant? Because someone of his status carrying a ladder would have made no sense."

"Perhaps," Maude conceded. "But you must remember it was a night of celebration, so very few were paying attention." She shrugged. "Besides, we did our best to keep everyone away."

"You did?"

"Well, of course, dear." Maude wore a smitten little grin that had seemed permanently fixed on her face since she walked in. "Blake and I were well aware of what was going on, seeing how Laurence asked us if we had the supplies. And if so, could he use them at a cost?"

More baffled by the moment, Abby kept frowning. "And did that not strike you as unusual?"

"Rather the opposite when he explained his reasoning. How he feared you might try climbing the vine beside your balcony." Prudence wore the same silly grin as Maude. "As I was there at the time, it struck us as heroic, not to mention thoughtful."

"Indeed." Isabella grinned. "As I was there too."

"And me," Margaret chimed in, hand to heart. "And how intense he was about searching out the wood. If I did not know better, he would have ridden out last night in search of it, had it not been available. Perhaps even chopped down a tree." Her grin matched the others when she looked at them. "Am I wrong, ladies?"

Everyone shook their heads.

"Well, the ladder needs to go." She planted her fists on her hips. "As does the drunken man in my bed."

"Oh, I don't know if I would rush that." Prudence's eyes twinkled. "When I suspect it is only a matter of time before he ends up there, anyway."

"Sister," she exclaimed. "We are not even married!"

"But you will be."

"Not to him."

Maude's eyes twinkled as well. "Even though he is your hero?"

"Heroes do not defend others while intoxicated."

"I cannot quite blame him. He was most distressed over what you nearly did." Prudence's smile faded, and she grew rather serious. "Humor aside, I knew you were coming out to think things over, but had I known you meant to climb a vine, I would have stopped you. What were you *thinking?*"

"Laurence did not tell you?"

"No, but he made clear you were close to doing it," Isabella said. "Close enough that it truly upset him. Enough he requested whisky while he worked and built quite the ladder. I must say, his workmanship is excellent."

While she appreciated his discretion with her sisters and friends, he had, as a whole, been rather obvious about the whole affair when he pulled this stunt.

"Whatever his intentions, the ladder must be removed lest tongues start wagging." She rounded her eyes. "As does the man who built it."

Unfortunately, as it turned out, that request would not go nearly as hoped.

Chapter Ten

LAURENCE CRACKED OPEN one eye, then the other, and tried to figure out where he was. He frowned and sat up, grateful for the water on the bedside table. Assessing his situation, he downed it in three long gulps. His shoes were lined up neatly, and sunlight shone through the crack between curtains that led out to a balcony.

That's when he remembered.

He gazed around again and realized this was Abby's room. Her bed. He sighed in relief when he realized he was fully clothed yet flinched when flashes of kissing her returned. Enough to know he had not been fully present in a moment that had been so very important. That was not how he would have wanted their first kiss to go.

While tempted to leave via the balcony, people were up and about outside, so it would be best to sneak out the door and find his way to his room undetected. Fortunately, all was quiet when he peeked out, and he made it there without anyone being the wiser. A brief ring of the bell later, Harold arrived, followed by a tub and bath water.

"Good man," he praised, grateful for Harold's forward thinking. The moment the maids filled the bath and left them alone, he perked a brow at his valet. "What are you hearing below stairs? Above stairs? Have you seen Abby?"

"Other than speculation over new castle renovations below stairs, gossip remains relatively tame thus far, sir," Harold reported. "Gossip about Lady Somerset vanishing so early from her own ball is more prevalent."

"And the gossip above stairs?"

"The same," he said. "To the best of my knowledge, the only ones who are aware you ended up in Lady Somerset's bed are her friends, sisters, and naturally, her lady's maid, Eleanor."

"That many?" Which meant their husbands likely knew too. "I hope they realize nothing untoward happened."

"They do." Harold seemed hesitant but rallied on. "Clearly, you would not have been up to the task, sir."

Hell. "And they knew that how?"

"Because Lady Somerset and her sisters tried to wake you to remove you from her room, but you were quite unrousable."

He imagined he was.

"And you know this because I assume you were summoned?"

"I was." Harold nodded once. "And can confirm you were in quite a deep sleep."

"So what happened next?" he wondered. "And how was Lady Somerset's mood when she discovered me so immovable?"

"Quite distressed if I were to be honest," his man said. "She requested that water be left at your side and that you seek her out once you woke and were presentable."

So she had wanted the water left? He could only hope that meant he had softened her heart some.

"Very well." He gestured that Harold be on his way. "I will summon you again when I'm ready to dress."

Something he meant to take his time about, but he was most eager to see her again and apologize for ending up where he had. Better still, for kissing her in such a condition. It was one thing to build her a ladder and watch over her. It was another thing entirely to become intoxicated when such behavior never accomplished much of anything. Certainly not in business, and undoubtedly not with a woman. Especially one he wanted to make his wife.

As it happened, he found her in one of the smaller rooms downstairs doing needlework with her sisters and friends. She looked lovely as always, if not a tad drawn. While he could admit he would have preferred to find her alone, it was best to face the lot of them and get this over with.

"Ah, good afternoon, Mr. Wright." Maude smiled gaily at him. "We wondered if we might see you before supper."

"I fear I owe you an apology," he began, only for Prudence to shake her head and stand along with the others.

"You owe us no such thing, Laurence." She gestured at where she had been sitting beside Abby. "Fresh tea has just been brought in. Sit and enjoy it with my sister, then be sure to join us to dine in a bit."

While he might have chosen a spot farther away, he took Prudence's suggestion and sat beside Abby. Although she seemed unsettled by his proximity, she was not as cold as he would have imagined because she set aside her needlework and poured him a cup of tea.

"I take it you slept well?" She handed him the cup, her expression hard to read. "More so, that you found your way back to your room discreetly once you woke?"

"I did on both counts." He had debated how to go about this and decided honesty was best. "My apologies for last night, Abigail. I only had the best of intentions."

"I believe you did," she said, surprising him. "And for that, I thank you." She gave him a pointed look. "I would, however, request you not attempt climbing a ladder again when inebriated. Nor sleep outside when it is so cold." His heart skipped a beat when her voice softened like velvet and brushed his ear with warm concern. "You might have hurt yourself, Laurence."

"It shall not happen again. You have my word." Not only was he not in trouble, but she was calling him by his given name? *What wonders.* "As drinking heavily is not in my nature."

"I would hope not." She sipped her tea and eyed him. "Why

did you do it? Why build that ladder? Why drink so much while doing it?"

While he knew he had told her the night before, or early this morning as it were, he suspected she wanted to see if he would provide the same answer sober. Although tempted to be vague, he was the opposite.

"The ladder was meant to keep you safe lest you tried to conquer that vine again," he revealed, sipping his tea before he went on. "As to drinking, I suppose it was a way to cope with how sad you were at the bottom of the vine. Moreover, that I had inadvertently put you in the same situation as your late husband. If that were not enough, I did so because I have, unfortunately, become much like my father."

Abby seemed caught off guard that he would be so forthright. "And what kind of man was your father?"

"A ruthless one." He frowned, stared at the fire, and told her more than intended yet again. "Truth be told, he was less like a father and more like a battle commander. He was not the sort one wanted to defy or disappoint. Especially if one was his son. So, I did my best to emulate him and become someone he would be proud of rather than end up on the other side of his wrath."

"My goodness," she said softly. "I am so sorry to hear that but glad you shared such. Glad you felt comfortable enough to do so."

"I admit I did not." He turned his attention back to her. "But I realize the only way for you to truly desire marrying me is if you understand me better. Know me better. Yet with that comes a warning because I have never spoken of my childhood. I would have found it a weakness even days ago. However, last night, I realized just how much he's burrowed his way inside me. How much I have come to think like him not just in business but with women." He shook his head. "And that is not a place you or any woman deserves to be."

"That seems a rather large leap for you to realize simply because you came across me at the base of a vine when not at my best."

"I would say you were a tad worse than not at your best." Although tempted to touch her cheek, he held back. "You were genuinely struggling, Abby. To the point you nearly tried to climb a vine that, had you fallen, could have hurt you a great deal." He tilted his head in question and tried not to be upset with her when that was the last thing she needed right now. "Do you have any idea how difficult that climb would have been?"

"I do not," she said softly. "So, despite my embarrassment, I am glad you came when you did. That you were so concerned about me when what we have shared thus far certainly did not warrant it."

"Because what we shared is not nearly what it should be yet." He never looked away from her lovely face. Hoped she understood how genuine he was. "Not what I hope it will be. *Should* be. And that, despite how difficult for us both, needs to be done with more honesty. With a past put behind us, and a future where we know each other far better." He shook his head. "I have gone about things all wrong and intend to rectify it. Intend to get to know you rather than merely desire you."

She seemed unsure how to respond at first until she offered a small nod. "While I admit I remain wary of your true intentions, I suppose if we are to travel together, it would be recommended."

"It would." Although hesitant to bring it up, he needed to set something straight. "I might be hazy on some of this morning's details, but I have had flashes of kissing you, Abigail." He frowned. "And I have never been sorrier." He shook his head again. "Our first time should not have been like that. Rather, it should have been with us both fully present. You deserved better than a haphazard, drunken kiss."

Her cheeks turned rosy. "I quite agree."

He sensed she wanted to say more but held back, and that was probably for the best. If he started dwelling on what he remembered of that kiss, he might lose focus of his objective. Or, better put, what he really wanted from her, and he found it rather shocking.

"Stolen, untimely kisses aside," he held up his teacup, "I propose a toast to a truce of sorts, so we might see if we can form a friendship?"

She searched his eyes for a moment. "Truly?"

"Yes, truly."

Although clearly reluctant and perhaps even wary, it seemed she was indeed an adventurer at heart because she finally held her cup up as well. "Then I say we give it a go."

And so, they did that very afternoon right where they were, chatting until dinner was served. Then they chatted even more. In fact, they talked so much that neither noticed everyone drifting off to play cards and listen to music after eating. Nor did they realize the servants had cleared the table around them, leaving only refreshed beverages.

God's truth, he had never spent so much time talking with a woman, not only because his father's voice in his head would have shunned it before but because he rarely found they had much to say. Abby, however, had a lot to say about many things. Better still, he found everything she uttered interesting. Her passion for all things was enthralling. She might be beautiful and adventurous, but she was also intelligent and imaginative. Rather than take things at face value, she urged him to share more and talk about his various businesses so she might better understand them.

"So, you learn things hands-on before deciding to run a business?" she said when they finally left the dining room. It was so late that most had already gone to sleep. "That is how you knew how to build a ladder?"

"Indeed." He smiled. "I enjoy woodworking, so I invested heavily in carpentry trades. Everything from real estate to shipbuilding. I find the best way to understand a business is to understand what your employees do for you first. Their needs. Then, from there, tackle the business end of things."

"Hence your interest in speaking with Charles," she said as he escorted her to her room. "As much as I thought it a foolish pursuit, I feel quite the opposite now. I think he will benefit from what you have to offer, and you, in turn, will benefit from him."

"I can only hope." He considered her. "If Charles agrees to my visit, Jacob has requested I travel with you in a few weeks when you visit Lord and Lady Newcastle, but I wanted to ask you first. If you would prefer, I can travel separately."

"No," she replied, swiftly enough to satisfy him. Even better, she appeared to see things in a most businesslike manner. "I think it better we arrive in the same carriage, so Charles sees us as a unified front."

"Are you sure?" he asked when they arrived at her door.

"I am."

"Then I leave you to a good night's rest, my lady." While tempted to kiss her cheek, and better yet, her mouth, he was determined to do this right. So, he bowed at the waist and smiled warmly. "I had a lovely evening, Abigail, and look forward to talking more."

"As do I." A small smile curled her mouth. "Sleep well, Laurence."

Then she vanished inside her room and closed the door.

The same door she closed over the next few weeks after they'd spent ample time together. Days full of interesting conversations and good times with her friends and family. Moments that had him seeing her far differently than he had those first few days. She had promised not to climb the vine, so his ladder had been put away for now but not indefinitely, as he had a grand plan for it.

"You seem much changed, Mr. Wright," Harold noticed as he readied him to go down to supper. They would be leaving for Charles and Grace's estate in the morning. "I take it you continue enjoying Lady Somerset's company?

"Very much so." He grinned. "Did you know she laughs?" Having marveled at the sound, he shook his head. "Really, truly laughs?"

A small smile hovered on Harold's mouth. "I did, as I have heard her laugh often."

"You say so, but I imagine you have not heard her laughter at its best." He kept grinning at his man. "Heard it when it's meant only for you because of something you said. How it feels when she smiles at you and only you." He shook his head. "I have never felt or seen anything like it."

"Without a doubt." Harold adjusted Laurence's cravat. "I am glad you enjoy her laughter, for I suspect she enjoys yours just as much."

"I cannot say." He eyed his friend. "Have I laughed that much?"

"Far more than I am used to." Harold nodded. "So, I would say yes."

He could understand why, given how upbeat he had felt these past few weeks. Friendship had come naturally to him and Abby. So flawlessly, he wondered how he'd ever been without it. Truthfully, he had never enjoyed another's company as much as hers. Not even Blake and Joseph's.

"Do you think Lady Somerset will like what I have planned for her tonight?" he wondered, worried yet again. "Or will she think it presumptuous? One step too far too soon?"

"I think she shall find it quite the adventure, sir." Harold grinned. "And Miss Eleanor agrees."

"Does she?"

"Indeed."

"I cannot help but notice you are spending a lot of time with Lady Somerset's maid." He eyed his friend curiously. "Might there be something to that?"

"It is too soon to say." Harold offered a small smile. "But perhaps."

"Good man." He clasped his valet's shoulder and nodded with approval. "Wishing you much success in winning her over."

As much success as he hoped he had with Abby.

"You seem quite happy this evening," Abby noted later that

night as they strolled arm-in-arm down a corridor leading toward the back of the castle. "Have I missed some tidbit of good news?"

He understood her asking because when he wasn't with her, he had secured a few promising business ventures with those unconcerned about whether he was part of the peerage or not.

"Nothing new." He met her smile. "I'm just happy. Happier than I can remember being in some time."

"Me too," she confessed. "The past few weeks have been surprisingly good." Her gaze lingered on him. "You have been surprising, Laurence. More surprising than I imagined."

"As have you, Abigail," he said softly. "Very much so."

She smiled and blushed prettily. "I think perhaps we have finally graduated to Abby."

"And yet again—" he met her smile—"you add to my happiness." Rather than turn back at the end of the hallway, he steered her down a narrow corridor. "That said, I wish to lend to your happiness as well if you are up to the challenge?"

Her brows swept up, and curiosity lit her eyes. "Do tell?"

"This is less about telling and more about showing." He offered her his hand. "But first, you must be willing to sneak me into your room." When uncertainty flared in her eyes, he shook his head and gave her a reassuring look. "Not for any nefarious reasons. I promise."

Where Abby would have adamantly denied him weeks ago, now she narrowed her eyes and smirked. "Are you sure as my room is a rather nefarious spot for you?"

"You have my word." He gestured ahead when Blake and Maude appeared. "To the point that Lord and Lady MacLauchlin will be present one way or another."

"How interesting." Abby met Maude's smile. "Care to share the great mystery?"

"If you dare to accept the challenge, you will know soon enough, sister." Maude gestured down another hallway. "This way will take you there discreetly, and then the rest is up to you."

Abby looked from them to him, thinking about it before she

shrugged. "Why not?"

Relieved she said so, he shrugged as well. "Why not, indeed?"

When he pulled her past Blake and Maude, only for the couple to remain behind, Abby frowned over her shoulder at them. "Are you coming?"

"No." Still smiling, Maude shook her head. "But we will be waiting, dear sister."

"More interesting still," Abby murmured, following him up.

"One moment," he said at the top of the candlelit stairs. He opened the door and looked left and right before pulling her after him until they were in her room, and the door closed behind them.

"I do not understand." She looked around in confusion. "Am I missing something?"

"Only those." He gestured at her bed. "Because wearing them is the only way you will be climbing down that ladder. A ladder that once again leans alongside your balcony."

Abby's eyebrows whipped up when she spied the trousers, tunic, light jacket, and sturdy ankle boots on the bed. They had talked about a lot over the past few weeks but, at her request, had steered clear of Reginald and the dynamics that had made her want to both escape and remain with him. She had told Laurence she would share more when she was ready, and he'd agreed to such. He understood entirely that she needed to take her time.

"Because you *do* still want to climb down that ladder, do you not, Abby?" he said softly. "Have ever since I built it?"

"That first night, I would have said no because it was too much." Her gaze lingered on the clothes. "But perhaps..."

"What?" he prompted gently when she kept staring. "What is it?"

"It is more than I expected," she managed hoarsely. "More than I might be ready for."

"Then do not do it." He slipped his hand into hers and shook his head. "Don't do it if you are not ready."

"How can you say that when you are not entirely sure what I

may or may not be ready for?" She didn't look at him in defiant anger like she would have weeks before but with a new type of curiosity. "We have not spoken of this to any extent, so you do not truly know."

"No, but I hope to." He gestured at the clothes again. "Until then, I suspect you need to conquer that ladder. Then, perhaps we will talk about things we have avoided until now."

"Perhaps." She squeezed his hand, then drifted to the clothes. "Who provided these?"

"Maude had them made based on the sizes Eleanor provided."

She looked at him in shock. "So my maid knows about this too?"

"She does and is quite excited for you."

Abby smiled. "She would be."

"She was under the impression you could manage your chemise around your stays." He cleared his throat. "But of course, if you need help, I will assist."

"You would have said that with an entirely different tone and look in your eyes weeks ago, Mr. Wright." Pink dusted Abby's cheeks when she glanced his way again. "But interestingly and no doubt purposely, I am in an overly manageable chemise this evening."

"Very well." Hope mixed with daring in his eyes. "So will you put on the clothing provided?" he asked. "Will you climb down the ladder so we might talk further?"

She hesitated for a stretch. Long enough to worry him that she might not be willing to take this step and find her way to him. If he had figured out nothing over the past few weeks, it was that Abby was an outstanding and complex woman. From how intensely she felt happiness and laughter to the sadness that flickered in her eyes when she thought no one was looking. A sadness he longed to get to the bottom of, not so he could marry into the peerage but because he wanted to free her from it.

"I will put them on," Abby whispered before she cleared her

throat and looked at him with determination. "And I will climb down that ladder."

"Good." He smiled and nodded once, sure to sound proud of her. "I'm glad to hear it." Rather than linger and give her a chance to back out, he headed for the balcony door. "I will be waiting outside."

Although tempted to look back and offer her an encouraging word, this moment needed to be hers. All hers. So, he stood outside and waited, hoping she would see this through. More than anything, though, he prayed she was willing to take the next step toward a future he suspected would be extraordinary.

Chapter Eleven

ABBY WAS NOT sure how she felt about everything that had happened since Laurence left her room the day after he slept on her balcony. Unsure what to make of the profound difference in him other than to pray it was not what she had feared.

That he was going about another method of attack when it came to making her his wife.

Because if he were, it was terribly effective. From the moment he'd sat down on the settee next to her weeks ago and apologized to this very moment. Now she was in limbo, staring down at trousers and a tunic made to her size. To a challenge that she face her past and tackle a feat she had wanted to confront the night he'd come across her crying, only in a much safer way.

As it turned out, Laurence had been every bit as terrifying as she knew he would be for no other reason than how drawn to him she had become. How much she'd come to long for his company and conversation, craving the unexpected friendship that had blossomed between them in so little time. A comradery she feared trusting because of how swiftly it had arrived. How new it felt.

Yet, it felt profound, too.

Extraordinarily real.

More genuine than any connection she had ever felt because of how well it ebbed and flowed. He might have been a superior businessman and dauntingly good at what he set his mind to, yet these aspects of him had seemed absent during their numerous conversations. All she felt in those was her. How he looked at her. Engaged her. The way he spoke freely about things men had never talked to her about.

How he had made her feel relevant.

Better still, how he'd made her feel like she could, at long last, truly thrive outside of the walls Reginald had so mightily erected. And she could. Would. *Had* to. Reginald might have feared it, but she need not anymore. Or so she prayed because she wanted to trust Laurence.

Love in a way she had never been allowed.

In a fashion, she'd been taught to distrust.

She fingered the clothing left for her and felt a jolt of excitement at the possibility of freedom beyond her wildest imagination. So, not debating a moment longer, she dressed, finding it odd but not altogether unpleasant to slip into trousers that fit her quite nicely.

While determined to storm out and finally make a mighty leap off her freedom balcony, she did not rush out as quickly as she might have thought. Instead, she stopped and gazed around at her room. Even though she would be back, she looked at everything as she had numerous times before, caught in the shadow of caring for Reginald. Then her gaze drifted to the balcony door like it had every visit. And every time, she'd fantasized about opening that door and stepping onto a balcony from another time. Perhaps stepping into a time when a doting, loving husband waited for her.

Moreover, when she ended up in a life denied her.

So, going with the fantasy, she inhaled deeply and nodded before opening the door and stepping out into the chilly night air. As though he had been standing there all along, in every memory of this balcony, Laurence smiled and did nothing more than wait for her next move.

He didn't touch her, or talk, but waited, and she could not be more grateful.

"This is all rather well-lit," she murmured, taking in the torchlight on her balcony. When she looked below, it was to more torches and Maude and Blake smiling up at her. She glanced at Laurence and could not help a small smile of her own. "You really did think of everything, did you not?"

"I had to," he said softly, not meeting her smile but instead acting most serious. "For you." His gaze swept over the balcony. "For what this means to you."

"Yet you still do not know what that is in its entirety," she reminded.

"No." He shook his head. "But you do, and that's all that matters."

She did, and he was right. This moment was not for him but for her. For the memories she had enjoyed with Reginald as well as those when she escaped onto this balcony and longed to climb down her vine. It was all tied together.

All part of the same bittersweet past.

One Laurence had given her a chance to confront head-on. And confront she would if it were the last thing she did. Confront before she ruminated about the past for one more moment. Not when she could finally leap over the edge and journey forth into the life she could have had if not for Reginald's careful nature and overzealous protection.

So, while not flying away by any means, she squared her shoulders and went to the edge to swing over, only to stop when she realized Maude and Blake were not alone. Prudence, Isabella, and Margaret were there too. Jacob, Joseph, and Robert were beside Blake and in positions to catch her if she fell, by the looks of it.

"Now, this is just embarrassing," she exclaimed, looking from Laurence to everyone below. "How bad a climber do you think me?"

"We do not care," Isabella called up. She grinned and shrugged. "All we care about is giving you this moment—but not at the expense of your life."

"Indeed." Margaret grinned as well. "To that end, I very much applaud Mr. Wright for thinking this all through quite thoroughly."

"As do I." Prudence nodded with approval, her gaze most loving when it locked with Abby's. "So, what are you waiting for, dear sister? Are you ready to finally take the plunge into a whole new world?"

"A whole new world, is it?" Yet she could not help but meet her sister's smile. She tried to get angry, she really did, but instead, she chuckled. Then, she outright laughed because it felt so good. Laughed because it felt freeing.

Something she had never dared do on this balcony.

Laughed until she was done laughing, then rallied her courage and stepped over the ledge onto the ladder, only to freeze when she realized how high it actually was. Froze when she realized the absurdity of what she was doing.

"I'm here." Laurence rested his hand over hers and looked her square in the eyes. "I will be with you every step of the way, Abby. Every step you take, whether it is away from this balcony or right back onto it."

Seeing how serious he was, she gripped the ladder tighter and wondered if it were not safer to rejoin him on the balcony. If it were not wiser, returning to the safety Reginald had assured her was necessary.

"It's all right, Abby," Laurence said softly. "It always has been."

"No," she whispered, closing her eyes to the pain. "It has not."

While understandable, it had never been all right. Not really. So she opened her eyes to Laurence's, glad for the steady support she saw in his gaze, then rallied forth.

It was time to face this.

Time to take the metaphorical leap she had too often dreamt about. So, without giving it another thought, she never looked back and climbed down a wall that had begun to epitomize her and Reginald's marriage. Although saddened, she felt freed by every step she took. She breathed in the ever-freshening air and felt lighter wrung by wrung. Less frightened and bolder. Excited. Almost as if chains around her ankles fell away. As though everything weighing her down melted away until she felt the cold, hard ground beneath her feet.

Startled, she glanced left and right only to find her sisters and friends there smiling. She had *made* it. *Done* it. She'd finally jumped off her freedom balcony. Took the plunge and landed on her own two feet.

Yet something was lacking.

As happy as she was to see her friends, she looked up and locked eyes with Laurence, who leaned against the ladder at the top to ensure it remained secure. Laurence, who grinned and eyed her proudly. A foolish American who had built a ladder to make sure she escaped one life and landed in another.

Even if he were playing at some sort of game at this point, it had become a very welcome one, at least for this. For now. How she felt when she met Laurence's smile and gestured that he climbed down too. Rather than step away, she kept her weight on the ladder until he was nearly to her and then pulled away.

"So?" Maude looked at Abby and grinned from ear to ear. "How do you feel, sister? Do you want to climb back up or—"

"No." Abby shook her head, eyed the balcony above, and felt the opposite of what she had felt weeks ago standing at the base of the vine. She no longer felt like she needed to prove something to herself. More than that, she was much closer to letting go of a relationship that, while caring in its own unique way, had been terribly binding. Instead, she was edging toward wanting to run in the opposite direction. To be young. Free. Taste life for the first time. "I really, truly do not want to climb back up."

"Then do not." Having made it safely to the ground, Laurence bowed from the waist, smiled, and held out his hand. "I have one more thing to show you tonight if you are game?"

Curious about what they thought of all this, she looked everyone's way only to find them vanishing into the night. All of them, Maude, Prudence, Blake, gone as swiftly as they had appeared to rally her on.

"Abby?" Laurence wiggled his elbow and smiled. "Shall we?"

Should she? Was it proper? Honestly, she could care less at the moment.

"Well, why not?" she said, slipping her arm into his. A position she had come to quite like.

"Where are we going?" she wondered as he led her alongside the castle, around a corner, then farther still. He grabbed a torch out of a wall bracket and glanced at her. "Are you ready?"

The way he considered her made her take pause. "I would like to think so."

"Then, follow me, my lady."

Curious, she followed him inside and up several flights of stairs until they arrived at another corridor.

"Here we are." Laurence opened the door to a lovely, spacious candlelit bedroom. "If you choose to accept it, welcome to your new room when you visit MacLauchlin Castle." He went inside, opened another door, and made a grand flourish outside. "And here is your new balcony, my lady."

"Oh my goodness," she whispered, eyeing the glorious chamber before she stepped out onto the balcony, and her breath caught.

Rather than looking up at trees, she looked down on them. The darkness of the woodland was not cloying but a vibrant carpet of greenery beneath a vast sky and a nearly full moon. It was gloriously windy and deliciously daring.

"This is perfect and most certainly speaks far more to freedom." Beyond touched, she blinked back tears when she looked at him. "Thank you, Laurence. This was very thoughtful. All of it, from start to finish."

"Yet, we are not quite finished." He vanished inside for a moment, then returned with flutes of champagne. "Not until we toast."

She smiled when he handed her a glass. "You thought of everything."

"I tried." He held up his glass. "Here is to new beginnings, Abby. Might your upcoming adventures be exciting, indeed."

"To new beginnings." Never so eager, she held up her glass as well. "And to new adventures."

They drank and stood beside each other, taking in the view.

"It really is something up here." She glanced over the edge. "Yet vine and ladder free."

"Which is likely a good thing at this height." He glanced over as well and considered things. "Not to say I would not find a way to scale it if I had to."

She meant to respond in a light-hearted tone but felt uneasy.

"May you never have to." She could not help a concerned frown because he was clearly a daredevil if given half the chance. "You would never, right, Laurence? Not when you need only knock on my door."

She didn't care how that sounded. The idea of him doing something so foolish terrified her.

"I would not," he assured her, smiling. "When the door truly is preferable." His voice dropped an octave. "Especially if you are on the other side."

Her skin warmed at the way he looked at her. The promise of not just friendship but more if she would have him. Far more. So much more she drifted closer, eager for a taste of it. For the adventure she saw in his all-encompassing gaze and the passion of which he was capable.

A passion that had been denied her for far too long.

"You said you wanted it to be a certain way the first time you kissed me," she said softly, nervous but excited all at once by how bold and forward she was. "Did you mean that? Did you—"

Laurence pressed a finger to her lips and set aside his glass. "Yes, I meant it." He set aside her glass, too, and cupped her cheek. "More than you can possibly imagine."

Caught between the warmth of his strong hand against her cool cheek and how tenderly he looked at her, she struggled for breath. Struggled to think clearly as he slowly reeled her against him and lowered his lips to hers. Where the first time, his kiss had been insistent and hungry, this go around, it was slow and passionate. So intoxicating she lost herself in it. Drowned in how heartfelt it seemed.

When his tongue touched hers like it had before, she felt just as intrigued. This time, however, he took it even further when his tongue danced around hers. If that were not heady enough, he made everything inside her spark to life when he angled his head even more and deepened the kiss. Even though she had never been kissed like this before, following his lead came naturally. So perfectly, she groaned before she could stop herself. Groaned when pleasure spiraled through her, and the same sweet ache he had evoked before between her thighs blossomed again.

Mortified she had made such a sound while kissing of all things, she pulled back abruptly and shook her head.

"What is it?" There was no missing the desire in his eyes. "Did you not enjoy that? Was it too—"

"It was perfect," she blurted and swallowed hard. More aware of him than ever, she struggled to find the right words. "I just…what I mean to say is I did not mean to groan like that."

"Why not?" He reeled her back into his arms before she went too far, wrapped his hand around the back of her neck, and eased her building tension. "There is nothing wrong with making sounds when you feel pleasure, Abby. It lets me know what you do and do not like. How to make you feel only pleasure all the time."

"Yet you did not groan," she noted breathlessly as he caressed the back of her neck, lulling her until she felt comfortable enough to say anything. "So, should I assume you did not like it as much?"

"You should assume the very opposite," he said a little gruffly, pulling her lower half more firmly against him. "I just express it differently."

Reginald had never held her like this and certainly never pointed out how hard he had become for her. Then again, she was fairly certain he'd never become so wickedly aroused. He'd certainly never made her feel what she did now.

"I want more," she whispered before she could stop herself, but she meant it. Needed it so badly she was rather surprised her legs still held her up. "I want all of it. All I can feel."

"Out of wedlock?" Laurence's pupils flared, and he tensed as though holding himself back. As if everything hinged on her response. *"Really?"*

"Yes, really." Prudence had done it, so why not Abby? It seemed the best of both worlds, in her opinion. Passion and freedom beyond the confines of marriage. Yet things must be made clear. "I want to experience what I never have. Feel what I never got a chance to feel. And I want it without obligation." She shook her head. "Lying with you will not lead to marrying you, Laurence." Quite adventurous, she thought about it and went on. "If anything, unlike in my previous marriage, it will let me know precisely what I will be in for if I become your wife. In turn, it would offer you the same."

"It would, indeed." Clearly intrigued, he issued a slow smile. "So you are not ready to dance with me yet, but you will lie with me?"

"The two are very different."

"They most certainly are."

"So, do you accept my proposal?" However nervous, she could not help a teasing smile. "Or would you prefer we draw up a contract?"

"Oh, that will not be necessary, my dear." He cupped her backside and squeezed her lower half more tightly against him. "Proposal accepted."

He looked at her with so much promise she knew the likelihood of her not enjoying everything he had to offer was slim to none. And it started the very moment he swept her into his arms, kicked the door shut behind them, and set her down beside the bed.

"Undress yourself, Abby, so I might watch you," he said softly, loosening his cravat.

"Here." She glanced at the privacy screen in the corner. "Might I not—"

"No, here." His smoldering gaze was quite predatory as he tossed aside his cravat. "I will help you with your stays, but this is your proposal, your adventure, so you should remain in control of it. I will undress you in all sorts of creative ways in the future if you decide you would like to do this again."

Somehow, based on that kiss alone, Abby suspected she would.

Having only ever worn a night rail beneath the blankets when Reginald mounted her, she rather liked the sound of removing her clothes. Liked the way Laurence watched her with unabashed anticipation when Reginald had refused to even look at her. So, however bashful, she offered a jerky nod and started undressing.

Something made all that much more marvelous because he did the same.

His body was so remarkably different than Reginald's that she could hardly focus on getting her shoes, coat, and shirt off. Therefore, she was rather clumsy about it. Never mind tackling her stays or trousers, of all things. All she could manage once half-undressed was staring at him wide-eyed, and who could blame her? Especially when he tossed aside his shirt, revealing a very fit form? Better still, when she saw clearly the hard, impressive ridge straining against his breeches?

"I think you forget this is your adventure." He stepped close and rested her hand against his hot, hard chest. His firm skin. "So, touch if you like."

"I would…" she breathed, resting her other hand on his chest. "Very much like to touch, that is."

Intrigued by the feel of him, his masculine strength, she ran her fingertips down the light smattering of hair on his chest, then over the hard ridges of his abdomen. Then, bold indeed, she ran them lower until she touched the rigid length below that made clear how much he desired her. She longed to feel it inside her with such vivid intensity she groaned once more.

"Kiss me again," she managed, her voice strained. "Kiss me until—"

He seemed to understand because he yanked her against him and kissed her, not slowly this time, but with the same sort of hunger he had that first night. Kissed her so deeply and with such intensity her knees buckled, but he caught her.

Fortunately, it appeared he understood what she needed because he took the reins, tossing her stays aside when she had not even realized he untied them. After that, seemingly as desperate as her, he removed their clothes in record time, even though their lips rarely separated. Ravenous for more of his kisses and reveling in the erotic sensation of his skin against hers when he lay her down and came over her, she spread her thighs and pressed against him. She needed the ever-growing ache between her thighs assuaged.

Caught somewhere between unbearable need and the intensifying pleasure invoked by how he touched and kissed her, everything faded away except him and how he made her feel. From the warmth of his lips to the feel of him caressing her breasts to the unbearable need ignited by him sliding his arousal back and forth over the sensitive flesh between her thighs without entering her.

The untouchable way he built her up without entering her.

Not just groaning but whimpering now, she moved with him as her pleasure grew. The ache went from throbbing to a sharp spearing sensation of near ecstasy that made her clench his arms tightly, arch against him, and cry out. She trembled and struggled for air as the sensation spanned out from her core and spiraled through her.

"What *was* that?" she eventually whispered when she finally found her voice. Laurence, meanwhile, seemed enraptured by merely watching her. "Did you feel the same?"

"That is just the beginning of how I intend to make you feel." He brushed his lips over hers. "And no, I did not feel what you did yet, but I did feel…" He struggled to find the words. "So much more than expected."

She had no chance to ask him what that meant before he kissed her, and she was once again lost in everything he pulled from her. Wondrous sensations she'd had no idea existed. Sensations that soon built her up all over again until she squirmed against him, desperate for more.

"You are so wonderfully responsive, love," he murmured against her lips before he cupped her cheek, and their gazes connected. That's when she saw just how entrenched he was in whatever this was overtaking them. How he was every bit as caught by her as she was by him. "Are you ready, Abby? Truly ready?"

"I am," she whispered because her voice was useless. "Beyond ready."

Where Reginald had plowed into her rather roughly, eager to get it over with, Laurence did the opposite. Instead, his touch remained tender, and his gaze never left her face as he gently pressed into her. Where this act had hurt before, it felt the complete opposite now. Rather, every small thrust forward felt better and better, but best of all was when he filled her entirely and released his own ragged groan of pleasure.

When she saw just how good she made him feel.

After that, it all became a blur as he kissed her again and moved. When she spread her thighs wider still and took him deeper. Felt a man the way a man was supposed to be felt. With incredible passion and heat and unending pleasure. In and out. Over and over. Sometimes slow, other times fast and hard and desperate. So much building and indescribable sensation that it was not long before she hovered on the edge again.

She hovered until he pressed deep, locked up against her, and released a long, low ragged groan that took her with him. Took her so intensely that she cried out in a soul-shattering release that told her just how much trouble she was in when it came to Laurence.

More so, she was well beyond trouble with no hope of return.

Chapter Twelve

LAURENCE ONLY KNEW one thing when he found such exquisite pleasure in Abby's arms: he would never, no matter what it took, let her go. Not with what he felt between them. How incredible they could make one another feel.

And he had been with enough women to know.

The moment he'd laid eyes on Abby in the tavern, he had suspected she was different, and he'd been right. She was beyond all the others. Far better. From whom she was as a person to the pleasure she felt and gave in bed. He had expected their first time to feel good, but this had been sensational. Transcendent, because he had not just felt it with his flesh, but—he feared—very much with his heart.

They had done little in the way of lovemaking and all its varying techniques, but it had not mattered in the slightest. Not when he'd watched her lose herself in his arms and lost himself in her, just as readily. Where he'd thought she would be bolder at the get-go because she was such a vivacious flirt by nature, it turned out there was a painfully innocent woman hiding beneath. One who almost seemed virginal when they undressed. It was as though she had never laid eyes on or touched a man before.

While he would be lying if he said he had not found that arousing, he wondered how often she'd suffered Reginald's touch because her actions tonight made it seem rarely. If anything, she had barely been touched at all. So perhaps it had just been a rutting thing for the old man?

Hard to believe with a woman like Abby.

She was built beautifully. A rare treasure to see when he removed her clothes. From her full breasts to her perfectly rounded backside, her soft, flawless flesh begged to be touched. If all that were not enough, she seemed to come alive at said touch. Every little caress evoked a response. A groan, moan, whimper, or cry. Even better, her varying unhindered expressions when receiving pleasure made a man feel like he had conquered the world. Made him strive to draw more sounds from her and see more ravishing responses.

"So what do you think?" she murmured after catching her breath. Her fingers trailed lazily down his sweat-slicked back, and her tight sheath kept milking him. "Shall we be trying this again at some point, or have we had our fill?"

He smiled because she clearly wanted to make love again. "I suspect we are nowhere near having had our fill."

Desperate for her taste again, he dropped several small kisses on her lips before, helpless to do anything else, he deepened the exchange. He was yet again pleasantly surprised by how well she did this. How perfectly aligned even their kisses felt. Everything about them, for that matter. To the point, he wanted it all. Every last bit of her and said so against her lips without realizing he had voiced it.

"What does that mean?" Her gaze returned to his face. "Because it sounds rather possessive."

"Not possessive."

It was, though, and he knew it, but he felt a sudden and very acute urgency no doubt born of his past. He could not fathom losing her, as his father had lost his mother. Lose her because he had not taken the time to truly know her. Care for every aspect of her. Yet how could he do that if she did not open up to him? If he did not have all his facts upfront, so he did not make the same mistakes as Reginald? Perhaps the same mistakes as his own father?

So, this needed to be addressed sooner rather than later.

Now, for that matter.

Although he would much rather stay where he was, he rolled off her, sat on the side of the bed, and looked at her most seriously. "I want to understand why you seemed so innocent tonight. What kind of marriage it was that you could show the world such happiness but still be so sad?"

"No real marriage at all." She seemed unsettled as she sat up as well. "I thought you were going to let me talk about this when I was ready? I should climb down my metaphorical ladder at my own pace?"

He had thought so, too, but found himself impatient and desperate in a way he didn't entirely understand. Worried if she did not conquer these last hurdles soon, then she might never. If that happened, what real chance did he have?

"I would think your moment to share more with me is here." He grabbed his trousers off the floor next to the bed and pulled them on. "Come and sit so we might talk." Laurence wrapped the blanket around her shoulders and gestured at the settee. "Unburden yourself, at last, Abby. Let the past go so we might have a future."

"I fear you have gotten ahead of yourself." Abby frowned and pulled the blanket more securely around herself as if suddenly uncomfortable in front of him. "We have no future as of yet, Laurence." She gestured at the bed, painfully blunt when he'd thought after what they had shared over the past few weeks and then, tonight, would have made a difference. "We have this, my contractual obligations, and what I had hoped was the start of a true friendship."

"You make it all sound so businesslike," he said dryly.

"Is that not what this is?"

"No, that is not what this is," he nearly bit back but held his tongue, feeling more and more uneasy by the moment. Like when he'd watched his mother turn from him and his father all over again. Felt a sense of loss that would never be replaced and untouchable pain he feared feeling again.

"I think I should go." He yanked on his shoes. "It has been a busy night. Best you get some rest."

"I agree." Her voice sounded strained. "Once again, thank you, Laurence…for everything."

"My pleasure." He did his best to ignore how unsettled and perhaps even wounded she looked as he offered a brief bow from the waist. "My lady."

In no mood to linger, he headed downstairs, trying to figure out how things had gone so terribly wrong so quickly. Why she had decided not to open up to him despite finding the courage to escape her freedom balcony. What he had done wrong.

Moreover, he could not help but wonder if his father had ever figured out how he'd wronged his mother. He knew his father had been a hard man, and that was likely the reason, but he had no proof. Having made a cuckold out of her husband, his mother had moved into one of their various homes and shut them out of her life before passing away.

Suffice it to say, Laurence was too restless and troubled to sleep all that long, so he got up early the next morning and worked up extra proposals for his meeting with Lord Newcastle. He kept his mind busy with various ideas he thought might suit the English businessman and did his best not to think of Abby and how she had felt in his arms. Refused to contemplate how much he'd come to care for her when she could very well turn him away in the end.

"Good morning," Prudence said as she and Jacob joined him downstairs for breakfast. A small, knowing smile hovered on her face when she glanced around. "I take it my sister is still abed?"

They were a presumptuous lot, weren't they? Truly, though, had their conversation gone differently last night, he and Abby would very likely still be wrapped up in one another's arms at this very moment. He fought back the regret that swamped his already damp spirits.

"I could not say where your sister is, Your Grace." He stood and bowed, then sat again. "I have not seen her since I showed her to her new room last night."

"My, how formal we have suddenly grown." Prudence eyed him as she and Jacob sat. "And did Abby like her room? Her new balcony?"

"I believe so." He was about to go on when Abby, who appeared rather drawn, joined them and sat beside Prudence rather than him. Even though he tried to catch her eye to gauge where they stood, she did not look his way. "But then, it seems you may ask her yourself."

"I was just asking Mr. Wright how you found your new room, dear sister?" Clearly noting they were not next to each other when they had been nearly inseparable over the past few weeks, Prudence glanced from him to Abby. "You must have been most impressed as Laurence picked it out. He thought it would be the perfect place to begin your new adventure and—"

"It was lovely." Abby nodded graciously at him without quite meeting his gaze. "Yet again, thank you, Mr. Wright."

So, they were back to that? Back to stiffly said last names. All because he wanted to finally hear the things she had not shared yet? Because he wanted to help her navigate whatever Reginald had done to her?

"Oh, dear, formal indeed." Prudence glanced at Jacob and flinched before looking back and forth between Laurence and Abby again. "What happened? Because I loathe seeing you both like this when you are so very good for each other."

"Sister," Abby muttered, obviously not pleased Prudence had been so forthright.

"What?" Prudence exclaimed. "Am I wrong that you and Laurence were getting along famously? That you were becoming fast friends?"

"We were, but now we are not," Abby said bluntly, surprising him with how sharp she was about it. Vehement even. "I will see through my obligations to Mr. Wright, and then, as I have said all along, we shall go our separate ways."

"Good gracious." Prudence's eyes narrowed on him enough to tell him she blamed him for whatever this was. "I cannot imagine why, but trust it is for a good reason, sister."

Not about to be accused of some villainous thing he did not do, he made things clear whether Abby liked it or not.

"Imagine all you like, Your Grace, but it is *not* for a good reason," he said. "Unless one considers that a friend who wants to understand Abby's previous marriage better and why it took a ladder to finally escape it, a good reason. For that is what caused her change of heart. My singular crime."

Based on her hardened expression, Abby was about to reply with something derogatory, but Finlay announced their carriage was ready for travel after they finished breakfast.

"Thank you, Finlay." Jacob gestured at Abby that she should reply to Laurence. "Do carry on."

"I would rather not." She did not bother looking Laurence's way. "In fact, I fear Mr. Wright and I have nothing further to say."

"I could not agree more." Having lost any appetite he'd been able to muster, he stood. "As you made that quite clear last night." He bowed to Jacob and Prudence. "I shall see you in the carriage."

Feeling both angry and desperate, emotions that would not suit a day of business, he thanked Finlay for his coat and hat, then stepped outside and struggled to clear his mind. Harden his heart. He inhaled the cold air and saw only what he hoped to achieve.

Not a marriage, but the money to be made.

Thankfully, he did not have to wait all that long before the others joined him, and they were on their way, with their servants in a carriage behind them. Although Prudence and Jacob chatted quite a bit, he and Abby, who had no choice but to sit beside one another, remained silent. He found their silence unfortunate, too, because he had been looking forward to this trip and eager to travel with her outside of the MacLauchlin Castle walls.

"While I am glad to have you along and know you are eager to meet our new niece—" Prudence said to Abby a few hours later when an impressive English castle on a seaside cliff loomed in the distance—"are you quite ready for this?"

"I would hope so, considering I have come this far, sister." Abby sighed and gazed out at the castle. "But yes, I am ready. What happened here is behind me now."

When he frowned at Prudence in confusion, her eyebrows whipped up. "Dear me, you did not tell Laurence about your history with this castle, Abby?"

"Why would I, when it is none of his concern?"

"Because I suspect he would have liked to know." Prudence's voice gentled as she looked from Laurence to the castle. "You see, Abby's late husband Reginald passed away in this castle's great hall when last she visited. Died quite abruptly and right in front of her, I am afraid."

"Good God." He frowned at Abby, but she only stared out the window. "Your sister is right. That is something I would have very much liked to have known. I'm so sorry, Abby." He reached out to touch her—something he would have done so easily only a few hours earlier, but now, he didn't dare.

"Lady Somerset," she said tightly.

"Abigail and nothing less," he groused before he could stop himself. Damn her for pushing him so far away when she needed him most. He might be upset with her, but he very much cared about her well-being. "If you need to talk or—"

"I do not, nor will I."

When he glanced at Prudence and Jacob for any kind of assistance, they only offered sympathetic looks in return. He was on his own. Very much on his own because he suspected Abby had not even let her sisters into the depths of her relationship with Reginald.

"Ah, they must have seen us approaching." Prudence grinned when she spied the couple coming down the front steps as their carriage pulled up.

"My dear, lovely sisters," exclaimed a beautiful blonde who could only be Grace, the moment they stepped from the carriage. She embraced both Abby and Prudence at once. "How absolutely wonderful that you have come to visit." The three held on tightly before Grace pulled back, squeezed Abby's shoulder and looked at her with concern. "I thought perhaps you may never want to return here, given the circumstances."

"Of course, I was going to return," Abby said. "One must confront these things, yes?"

She could have fooled him last night. Or even today.

"I suppose they must." Grace turned a gentle smile his way. "And you must be the American heir we have heard so much about. Mr. Wright, I presume?"

"Yes." He bowed at the waist. "It is a pleasure to finally meet you, Lady Newcastle."

"Indeed, it is." She gestured at the sizeable man beside her. An imposing sort, even taller than Laurence, and with a patch and scarred cheek, there could be no doubt he had seen his fair share of battle. The fact it was against Laurence's countrymen was unfortunate. "Mr. Wright, my husband Charles, the Earl of Newcastle."

"A pleasure to meet you, Lord Newcastle." He bowed again. "I appreciate your hospitality and look forward to speaking with you further."

"And I, you," Charles replied, not stiffly but not precisely with warmth either. "Welcome to my home. I look forward to talking business once we have enjoyed refreshments."

Jacob gave Laurence an encouraging look as the sisters linked arms and made their way up the stairs. Where MacLauchlin Castle had a welcoming feel about it, this one seemed more weatherworn and confrontational. As though it had seen hard times, but persevered.

When Abby slowed upon entering the great hall, and her gaze lingered sadly on the floor, he wanted to comfort her. Rest her head against his chest and let her know he was here for her. Unfortunately, however, he could not when she only pushed him away more by the moment.

"Come, sister." Grace steered her into a drawing room every bit as impressive as the great hall had been. "Let us enjoy something a tad stronger than tea, perhaps?"

"I think perhaps that would be wise." Abby's voice shook just enough to let him know how distressed she had become. "Then straight up to see your little one if she is awake, as I am eager to finally meet her."

"Of course." Grace urged her to sit on one of two sofas facing each other in front of a crackling fire and sat beside her. "Until then, how are you doing? Letters say much, but they do not let me see your face. Disallow me from gauging how well you actually are."

"I *am* well," Abby assured, once again avoiding eye contact with him when he sat across from her. She smiled at Grace. "Truly, darling. Really very well."

Clearly as cued into Abby as Prudence had been, Grace glanced from him back to her sister as though sensing the tension between them.

"All right then." Grace smiled kindly at the servant who delivered a tray of refreshments. "Then let us catch up." She exchanged an imploring glance with Charles. "If it is just the same, I think perhaps some time alone with my sisters sooner rather than later is called for?"

"Of course." Charles eyed Laurence's scroll case. "It seems our new American friend is ready to get down to business anyway."

He knew it uncouth to have brought his paperwork in so soon, but proper British manners were not his way of going about things. Business was business, and he preferred dealing with it earlier in the day before alcohol started flowing. He preferred clear minds and smart decisions.

To that end, after Charles led them down a corridor lined

with dour-looking patriarchs into a study, he turned down good Scottish whisky from Blake's distillery in favor of tea and was glad to see Charles do the same. Even so, he would not proceed until they addressed what could strain their working relationship going forward.

"I prefer to be forthright with those I am considering going into business with, Lord Newcastle." He sat beside Jacob across from Charles at a desk as impressive as its master and watched the Englishman closely. "That said, I did not support the war in which you fought. I did not think we should have been involved. And while I will not apologize for my countrymen's actions, as I am a proud American and they but soldiers following orders, I will apologize for your suffering. For the suffering of every soldier who fought in the war on all sides in every country. For the wounded and lost. For the wives and children who suffered those losses. The brothers, sisters, aunts, and uncles who will never see their loved ones again."

He paused a moment, letting that sink in before continuing.

"It is my fondest hope that you understand everything I have just said before we move forward," he said, brutally honest because this situation was more precarious than most. "I need to know you will not let your past and feelings toward Americans affect what we might accomplish together. That you will not let it hold sway over important decisions. If for even a moment you think it might, be honest now and save us both a lot of wasted time." He shook his head. "I will not fault you for it but rather be grateful for your honesty."

Charles said nothing at first but merely sat with his arms crossed over his chest, contemplating Laurence in a way that likely intimated most but not him. He had sat across from men like this often enough. Let them size him up while he did the same. The only difference with Charles was how affected he had been both inside and outside by Laurence's countrymen.

When Newcastle finally spoke, he was as direct as Laurence. "How much did Jacob and Blake tell you about me?"

"Enough to know you suffered indeed," he replied. "But more importantly, enough to assure me you are well on your way to recovery. That your mind remains less and less in battle these days and more in the present."

Still showing no outward sign of his thoughts, Charles glanced from Jacob to Laurence and contemplated him further before, at last, he unfolded his arms, rested his hands on the desk, and gave him his answer.

Chapter Thirteen

"TALK TO US, Abby," Grace said softly after the men adjoined to the study to talk business. "Tell us what is going on. How you truly feel about being here." She glanced from Prudence back to Abby. "Because I was rather counting on this incredible new friendship, I hear you share with our American to soften the blow of returning, yet you and Laurence are clearly at odds."

She went to respond that she was perfectly fine but ended up biting back a sob.

"Oh, dear." Prudence set down her tea and sat on Abby's other side. "What is it, darling? Is it Reginald? Are you missing him?"

She nodded. "Yes." Then shook her head. "And no." She nodded again. "But still, yes, somehow."

"Because you are back here?" Grace said.

"Partly." She bit back another sob. "But mostly not."

"Goodness." Grace handed her a handkerchief and urged her to rest her head on her shoulder while Prudence rubbed her back. "Then best you have a good cry and let all those yes's, no's, partly's, and mostly's out, love."

She tried to control her emotions but could not stop the tears once they started flowing, and she did indeed have a good cry. Not over Reginald but Laurence and how upset she was with him. How he had made a mess of things so swiftly after she'd realized her foolish heart had gone and fallen in love with him. She'd known it with such certainty when they made love that she was shocked she had not figured it out sooner.

In truth, she wondered if some part of her heart hadn't been his from the moment she bumped into him in the tavern.

Eventually, her tears subsided, and she nodded thanks when Prudence pressed a warm cup of tea into her hand and urged her to drink.

"Do you want to talk about it?" Grace said softly, gently coaxing. "Him...whoever that *him* may be?"

Implying they both knew precisely which *him* had her in tears. She had not told her sisters the dynamics of her relationship with Reginald, so telling them why she'd grown so upset with Laurence would likely ring shallow. All she could share was a version of it. The coating on a much deeper truth she should finally let them in on but, for some reason, could not because she feared their ridicule. Worried they might think her foolish.

"Tell us," Prudence prompted, seeing right through her. "What is it, Abby? What is that sadness in your eyes you show so rarely? That you think we do not catch?" When she shook her head in denial, her sister squeezed her hand. "Because it is not a new sadness by any means."

"It is just sadness over Reginald and," she began only to trail off when she nearly said what made sense. Him dying in this castle and how it felt to return here and see the very spot where he had breathed his last breath. The blasphemous freedom she'd felt mixed with horror because she *had* cared for him. Had loved him in some strange way but, at the same time, hated him.

"No." She swallowed hard, shook her head, and looked from sister to sister. "While yes, I miss Reginald for the friendship we found at the end, I loathe him for all he took from me. Not just being married to a man my own age and all that entails but the fear he instilled in me because of what he watched his daughter suffer."

"I had quite forgotten about her." Grace frowned and narrowed her eyes. "The poor thing died far too young if I recall correctly?"

"Though before our time, she died not all that much older than I was when I married Reginald," Abby managed. "Moreover, he singled me out because my vivacious spirit, as he called it, reminded him of her."

"Oh, dear *Lord*." Disgust flared in Prudence's eyes. "Please tell me he did not have some sort of sick perversion?"

Confused momentarily, she frowned before realizing what her sister meant. "Goodness, no, nothing like that. I look nothing like her, and he did not view me in a father-daughter fashion." She sighed. "Rather, the moment he saw my general disposition at my coming-out ball, I became a mission of sorts. You see, he meant to save me, as it were."

Grace choked a little on her tea. "Come again?" She met Abby's frown. "How does one save a girl who is one-third his age?"

"By making sure she did not end up like his beloved daughter."

However hard to share, it was high time she confessed to someone. While she had thought that someone would be Laurence, he'd pushed her too soon. Worse yet, he seemed to have expected it in exchange for the intimacy they had shared. Then he'd had the nerve to get upset, which told her he had changed little from whom she'd originally thought him to be. He might have done all the right things lately, but he was still ruthless on the inside.

Still driven to take what he wanted when he wanted it.

"You see, Reginald wanted me as his wife so I would not end up like his deceased daughter," she went on. "So I would not end up married to a man who wooed her and seemed the perfect suitor only to become something entirely different behind closed doors."

"What happened?" Prudence's heart was in her eyes. "What

really happened to Reginald's daughter, Abby?"

"Not what everyone was led to believe because she did not die of illness." She blinked back tears and shook her head. "Rather, it seems she was beaten to…"

Grace shushed her and squeezed her other hand when she struggled to find the words. "We understand." Her sister seemed to gather herself before resting her free hand on Abby's shoulder. Gathered herself to hear the rest of a sordid tale she had been clueless about. "Go on, sweet sister. You have always presented such an upbeat persona, yet now I fear there was much more to it. A backstory, as it were."

"In the years before he became crippled, our persona in public was one thing, but in private, we were something altogether different," she confessed. "He was never cruel but certainly never loving as I was just something to be kept safe like a precious bauble on a shelf." While she meant to end it there, something about holding onto her sisters made it all come pouring out. "He laid with me once so it would be official. One thrust to see things through. It must have been a horrible deed for him, to be sure, as our age differences were too great."

She swallowed again and gathered herself before continuing.

"I could still be myself, open and happy, when around others, but never was I to dance at a ball with anyone other than him." She cringed at the thought of it. At how she had come to dread those dances. "Yet dance with him I must so all knew I was his…even though I was not." She shook her head. "And how very lonely that was. Lonely in ways I cannot convey."

A stunned silence fell when her words trailed off. Sadness saturated her sisters' eyes as they squeezed her hands tighter and gathered her closer, much-needed walls of support.

"I had always thought it was one way between you and Reginald," Prudence finally said, wiping away a tear. "The discomfort of suffering an old, mean man, but it seems quite the opposite yet somehow just as bad." She pressed her lips together as if fighting emotion before continuing. "Then there were those awful years after he lost his ability to walk."

"Those were rather our best years," she admitted. "It's hard to describe what it is to see one's pride and dignity stripped away. To see them so humbled and dependent on others to do things that had come so simply before. It has a way of removing any anger you might have felt toward them. Helps one to see mankind and our vulnerabilities in a different light."

"No doubt it does." Grace tucked an errant curl behind Abby's ear. "Yet, at the same time, no matter how kind your heart, it must have only added to your longing, darling. Made you cherish your freedom balcony when you had time alone on it. Any place private, for that matter, wherever you and Reginald were at the time."

"It did." She dabbed her cheeks. "More than you could possibly imagine."

"Honestly, it is a wonder the whole situation left you any zest for life in the least." Grace shook her head, marveling at it. "Yet how bubbly you seemed at times. You were able to outshine anyone in your presence."

"Yet all a show, I suspect," Prudence said softly, seeing it for what it was. "A means to show all, especially us, that she was not suffering." She considered Abby. "Perhaps it was a means to escape your loneliness?"

"Indeed." She sniffled a little and dabbed her cheeks again. "Perhaps a bit of both."

"And now?" Grace rubbed her back while Prudence provided a fresh handkerchief. "Is the happiness Maude shared in her letters about you all for show? Because she seemed to think it quite genuine when you spent time with Mr. Wright."

"Letters?" She arched her brows at Grace. "How many did she send you?"

"Enough that I have followed things quite readily," she said. "Right up until this morning when a letter about Mr. Wright's most recent attempts to woo you arrived." A small smile curved her mouth. "You know how Maude loves to gossip, especially when it comes to her matchmaking schemes, so do share. Was your happiness with Laurence genuine?"

"I imagine it was," she said on a sigh, her chest heavy again. "Most genuine, indeed."

"Then, you must tell us all of it, love," Prudence said. "You must tell us how you and Laurence became such fast friends, and he did such incredibly sweet things for you these past few weeks, yet now you want nothing to do with him. It does appear quite the leap in little time."

She thought about how much to tell them. How much was appropriate.

"Well, it is quite simple," she said. "As Laurence so rudely shared over breakfast, he wanted to further understand my relationship with Reginald. He failed to mention, however, that I wished to share more about my late husband at my own pace. Something I thought he understood, but it seemed not." She fumed just thinking about it. "And after everything we had just shared together. Everything we felt when we..."

She snapped her mouth shut when she realized what she had said. What she most certainly implied.

"Ah, yes," Prudence murmured, eyeing her with amusement. "Somehow, I felt things would lead there, considering his romantic actions last night. Then, if I were to be truthful, the intense exchange between you this morning seemed a lovers' quarrel, to be sure."

Her cheeks heated, and she shook her head. "I did not mean to imply that we—"

"Yet you did." Grace smiled warmly. "And I cannot tell you how happy I am to hear it, all things considered."

"Nor I," Prudence said. "And do not look so embarrassed, Abby. You know full well I enjoyed Jacob out of wedlock and would have continued to do so." She grinned with approval. "I dare say there is something to be said for the freedom of it, is there not? It was most needed in your case. Long overdue, if I were to be honest."

"I could not agree more." Grace wore the same sort of knowing, curious smile as Prudence when she looked at Abby. "So, what did you make of it, sweetheart? Was it all you might have imagined?"

"It was nothing like I imagined." While tempted to lie because she was not pleased with Laurence, she just could not do it. "It was far better." Her cheeks warmed again at the thought of how exceptional he had made her feel. "Most unexpected."

"Quite right." Prudence's smile widened. "Somehow, I suspected it might be that way between you. To that end, if you are unaware of them, I shall teach you about precautions you can take if you decide against bearing fruit. Unless Mr. Wright took his own precautions."

"A forthright conversation indeed," Abby exclaimed under her breath.

"And quite prudent," Grace said, once again agreeing with Prudence. "Unless, of course, you intend to give Laurence what he wants by agreeing to marry him." She shrugged and grinned. "In that case, I, for one, would not be opposed to more nieces and nephews."

"Nor I," Prudence echoed.

"Be that as it may," Abby clarified. "I do know how to take preventative measures. It was something Reginald insisted I learn lest his one thrust mistakenly 'bore fruit,' as you call it."

"Good Lord," Grace said softly. "So he thought to take your youth and the joy of ever having children?" She shivered. "I do not care for his reasons. That is criminal indeed." Her tone gentled as she contemplated Abby. "Yet let us not stray from what happened after you experienced a far more caring man for the first time. Because though you may not like to hear it, Laurence wanting to understand you better after having what some men might consider the ultimate goal with a woman truly bodes well."

"It very much does." Prudence tilted her head. "So why grow so angry, Abby? Surely it cannot simply be because he asked for something you were not ready to give?"

"It was how he asked it." She frowned and blinked back more blasted tears. "How he was every bit what Reginald warned me about."

"And that is what again, precisely?" Prudence's eyebrows pinched. "Because I was under the impression Laurence's singular goal was to free you of your past rather than abuse you in any way."

"Whilst imprisoning me once again by showing me how vulnerable one becomes when one's heart is involved," she said before she could stop herself. "And proving he can be any which way to accomplish his goals. Then, as Reginald warned when it came to men, Laurence inevitably reverted to his old, demanding ways afterward. Ways that could very well become more daunting going forward as it had been for Reginald's beloved daughter."

"And now it becomes clear." Grace rested her hand over her heart and beamed at Abby with happiness despite everything she had just said. "You have fallen in love with your American."

"I have not," she denied.

"But you have."

"Perhaps a tad bit," she managed, flooded by too many emotions at once for talk to come easily. Anger, sadness, and yes, even still, love. "Only for him to make demands of me the very moment I figured it out."

"Did you tell him, then?" Prudence asked.

"Well, no, but still," she replied. "It was right after lovemaking, so one would have thought he would have had better timing."

"Hmm." Prudence narrowed her eyes. "As far as I can tell, his timing has been spot on, so I cannot help but wonder if him asking you at such a juncture had more to do with him than you. If he cared nothing for understanding you better, he would not have built that ladder nor grown impatient at a most inopportune time."

"It *does* bespeak a man who might be growing desperate." Grace tapped the side of her teacup and considered the whole situation. "From what I've heard, Mr. Wright has been most driven about making you his wife one way or another." She narrowed her eyes in thought. "So why risk how far he has come with bad timing? And if it were bad timing, he strikes me the type to smooth things over straight away as he has quite the favorable set-up with you as is."

Abby frowned. "I cannot say I understand what either of you are suggesting."

"Love, darling." Prudence squeezed Abby's hand again. "Based on the way Laurence looks at you and his touching gestures of goodwill, I suspect that, like you, he grapples with something quite unfamiliar to him." She shrugged. "I might be wrong, but I doubt he's ever been in love. And if he has, I think perhaps what he feels for you is even stronger."

Her chest did that odd tightening thing again, and breathing became a touch more difficult. "That is a lot to glean from very little."

"Even so." Grace nodded. "I agree with Prudence and have only known him mere minutes."

"Then truly, you know nothing."

"Unless one assessed him when you grew so sad upon entering the great hall," Grace countered. "And I did, only to find I liked what I saw. Liked how his concern for your well-being was genuine. Whether you saw it or not, it was there, Abby. I cannot say it was love, but it was profound and worth paying attention to." She sipped her tea. "Which, fortunately, you shall have time to do as you must step foot on a boat and travel somewhere with him still, right?"

"Plus, dance," Prudence reminded. "Unless you waltzed last night unbeknownst to me?"

"I rather got the impression that might have been on his agenda," Abby admitted, blushing. "But I fear I chose to trade up one for the other."

"Oh, how delightful." Grace chuckled. "Good for you, dear sister. Good for you, indeed."

"Quite right." Prudence mulled it over. "Though I rather think a dance could not have hurt either. That it still remains a step you need to take, Abby."

She was about to respond when a light rap came at the door, and it was announced the children were ready to be received if they would like to spend time with them. To be expected, their son Alexander flourished in his new home with a new father, and their little girl, Cecelia, was utterly precious.

"She is beautiful, Grace." Abby smiled down at the baby. "Such a perfect little darling."

Cecelia smiled in return, wrapped her tiny hand around Abby's finger, and gurgled happily, claiming the world as hers already. That, in turn, made her acutely aware of how much she would have liked to have a child of her own. Sadly, she had long given up hope such might happen.

"You are a natural with her, love," Grace praised, laughing. "Then again, it seems you two have similar personalities." She offered Abby a reassuring smile. "And you do still have a wonderfully vivacious spirit despite how forced things might have seemed over the years. Because let's not forget you were every bit as outgoing and loving prior to your marriage."

Abby supposed she had been however in the distant past it might seem.

If the truth be told, she was glad for the escape the children's visit brought. A break from such difficult conversations. Could her sisters be right about Laurence? Might he have come to love her too? If so, that almost made his persistence after the fact much more alarming. Made it far too similar to what Reginald had warned her about.

Eventually, lunch was served, and they retired to the dining room.

As it happened, only Jacob joined them, claiming Charles and Laurence were deep in discussion about Laurence's proposals and vice versa.

"It is hard to tell how well they will get on." Jacob smiled at everyone in reassurance. "But they certainly have a lot in common, thus a lot to talk about."

"I can only hope this is the beginning of a successful partnership and perhaps even a friendship." Grace met his smile. "I think such would be healing for Charles."

Jacob nodded. "I could not agree more."

"Well, then, we shall see a grand spread this evening for dinner, then a bit of gaming and dancing, perhaps." Grace smiled from sister to sister. "A chance for everyone to get to know one another and for you to enjoy the renovations we have made since last you were here."

"I cannot wait to see them," Abby said, quite taken with the old castle. Drawn to the whole area, for that matter. She had always loved England's northeastern shores when she visited. Loved the wildness of the sea.

"Very good," Grace said to Abby, quite excited. "Then, as soon as we finish eating, allow me to show you some of the first rooms we updated, as I do hope one will be yours when you visit."

"I would adore that, sister."

And she very much did until she realized how strategically located it was.

Chapter Fourteen

LAURENCE COULD ADMIT he liked Charles a great deal more than he thought he would. But then, he thought he would be dealing with a wounded war veteran who would not be able to see beyond his past to a successful future if it meant working with an American.

Never was he more wrong.

Or so it seemed thus far as he and Charles spent the greater part of the afternoon going over their various ideas and proposals, plus came up with a few new ones. If ever he'd met a kindred spirit when it came to business and improving everything he could, it was Lord Newcastle. They saw eye to eye on most things, and what they did not agree on, they hashed out until they came to an amicable, if not better, solution.

Eventually, both agreed to a glass of whisky to celebrate how much they had already accomplished and ended up getting to know one another on a more personal level. To the point Charles even spoke of his time in the Royal Navy and the battles he had fought. The suffering he had witnessed and how impactful Grace and Alexander had been on his life since then.

"Enemy though you were, it was a mighty fight on the American Navy's behalf," Charles admitted. "Many a battle well won."

"But a war more or less lost and a Royal Navy that more than proved its might, in my opinion." Remembering well the toll it had taken on his country, Laurence shook his head. "Good God, man, by the end of eighteen thirteen, you had established a commercial blockade that stopped all traffic across the entire east coast south of New England. Your navy did so well that the frigate *Constellation* never once managed to escape Norfolk throughout the war. You even kept the *Constitution* trapped in Boston Harbor." He took a swig of whisky and shook his head before continuing. "If that were not enough, you eventually extended your blockade to include New England."

"That was damning indeed," Charles agreed, taking a swig of whisky as well.

"It was." He frowned. "America's imports shrank by more than twenty-five percent. Then to add insult to injury, you marched on Washington, D.C., and burned down our capital."

Charles met his frown. "So we did."

Where Charles had tensed, clearly sensing a confrontation coming, Laurence gave him no such thing. Rather, lost to the past for a moment, he stared at the fire. "My father never cared a lick for the lives lost leading up to or during the war nor the soldiers fighting to protect him." He recalled what an especially ruthless monster he had become in those years. "His concern was only ever how the British affected his businesses and income. It was truly the most important thing in his life."

"And where did you stand at that time?" Charles wondered. "As I assume you did not enlist?"

"I did not because, again, I did not support the war." Laurence downed the rest of his whisky. "Though I admit now, part of me wishes I had enlisted. That I had ignored my father in my ear, saying fighting was for fools, that commerce was what made a nation." He met Charles's eyes. He looked at Charles most seriously. "In the vein of keeping things honest between us, I regret not having helped my countrymen when I could. For having allowed others to die for my freedom when I was young and able-bodied enough to fight."

"I appreciate your honesty." Charles seemed serious enough

before he shrugged and issued a small smile. "Though I can admit, given our current circumstances, both in business and in family, that I am glad we never met on the battlefield."

"Yes, that would have proven rather awkward, would it not?"

Charles chuckled. "Indeed." He held up the bottle of whisky. "Another?"

"As much as I would like to, I best not." He flinched. "I fear Lady Somerset has already witnessed me a tad too inebriated, and I will not have her see it again."

"Ah, yes, so I heard," Charles said, bemused. "Rumor has it you and Abby have already enjoyed quite the round of adventures with even more contracted on the horizon."

He sighed. "I can only hope."

"Is there trouble on the once calm seas, then?"

"Calm seas? Abby?" This time Laurence chuckled before his amusement faded. "But yes, so it seems, and I hope to get to the bottom of it if it's the last thing I do."

"Good." Seeming quite sure, Charles nodded. "She needs someone like you. I dare say, someone up to the challenge."

"A challenge to be sure," he said. "One I do not intend to fail at."

He had said that time and time again when it came to her, yet he felt more driven than ever now while, at the same time, never more uncertain. How else could he be when he felt things he'd never felt before? Emotions that made him doubt how to go about pursuing her now. All he knew was he wanted more than she was willing to offer. To see into her heart and understand her and Reginald. Every moment of their time together. Then, he did not want her to suffer what she had ever again. She needed to understand things would be different with him. He would make sure of it. Yet first, he needed her to let him in, so he understood what he was dealing with.

It was a conundrum he mulled over as Harold helped him prepare for dinner later that evening.

"How do I go about it, friend?" he wondered as Harold

tugged here and there at Laurence's evening coat, ensuring it sat just right across his shoulders. "How do I get Lady Somerset to finally tell me all her secrets? To allow me to care for her as I wish to care for her?"

"I do not know, sir." A twinkle lit Harold's eyes. "Although you are certainly close enough to her now to implement your strategy once you figure it out."

He arched his eyebrows. "Do go on."

"Well, it seems Lady Somerset was given the room beside yours." He gestured at the door in the far corner. "You even have an adjoining door."

"How convenient." Seeing the masterminds behind such a convenience, he grinned. "Well done, Lord and Lady Newcastle."

On more count than one, it seemed because, upon further inspection, he realized they had been given rooms with adjoining balconies overlooking the sea. Balconies high up, befitting Abby's ongoing break from the past and a blossoming sense of freedom. A wild side of the castle that most definitely suited her. Or at least it would when they were away from Reginald's influence once and for all. Because he'd become more and more certain her late husband had convinced her of all sorts of unsavory things.

As expected, she remained distant from him when he joined everyone in the drawing room before dinner. Yet as always, she was stunning in a simple, crème-colored dress with a subtle pearl necklace and earrings. How he longed to add to her collection of jewelry over the years. To fulfill her heart's every desire.

To lift the weight off her that had fallen so heavily over them last night.

Where Abby seemed vivacious as always while speaking to her family, she never once looked his way. Or so she wanted him to think; he caught her discreetly glancing over at him every so often. It was never long, but it was there.

While she directed no conversation his way, he was pleased when young Alexander did. Unlike Laurence's own relationship with his father, the one between Charles and Alexander appeared to be very good. If that were not enough, they seemed to share a warm friendship and an open, comfortable dialogue that undoubtedly encouraged Alexander to speak with Laurence. To see him not with prejudice but rather, curiosity and an open mind, which said much about Charles himself and how he viewed even those who should be his worst enemy. He also appreciated how often Charles and Grace allowed Alexander to join them in general. It was not common in America or England, and he thought it should be.

"So you are all the way from America, Mr. Wright?" Alexander asked, quite taken aback.

"I am." Laurence smiled. "And what do you make of that, Alexander?"

"I find it quite impressive." He tilted his head, curious. "How was the journey across the Atlantic Ocean? Did you enjoy a sturdy ship? Were the seas smooth or rough?"

"A bit of both, but I was on a sturdy ship," he said. "One I helped build, at that."

"*Truly?*" Alexander's blue eyes widened. "You can build ships?" Impressed, he glanced at Charles. "Did you hear that, Father?" His gaze flew back to Laurence. "Can you sail them as well?"

"I can," he confirmed. "In fact, I rather enjoy it."

"As do I." Alexander shrugged and grinned. "Well, Father is only just teaching me, but I believe I will master it in little time."

"I imagine you will." Laurence grinned as well. "For I can see you are driven to be sure." He nodded once with approval. "No doubt, a destined sailor."

"In my spare time for enjoyment, quite right." Alexander seemed rather determined. "For my profession, I intend to help design and build new structures whilst resurrecting old ones."

"Impressive," he granted. "So you will not simply be the next Earl of Newcastle and all that entails?"

"Goodness, no." Incredulous, Alexander looked from Charles to Laurence. "While I will most certainly serve my community, it seems better served still if I can contribute to it and England as a whole, does it not?"

"It does," he agreed, more impressed by the moment. "Perhaps someday you and I might go into business together, Alexander, as I dabble in real estate as well and look forward to seeing what you create."

Alexander's eyes lit with excitement before good manners and surprisingly good business sense got the better of him. He smoothed back the lock of white-blond hair that had flopped over one of his eyes and stood up a little straighter.

"I most appreciate that offer, Mr. Wright, and while I understand you are quite adept at building a ladder," he said studiously—invoking a slight choke on her tea from Abby—"I must ask that I see more evidence of your talent before agreeing to go into business with you in the future." He cleared his throat as though he had this all planned out, then continued. "To that end, given you know carpentry and building yourself, I thought you would carve something for me?"

"Of course," he said without hesitation. The lad was quite articulate and even more so, had the makings of a good businessman. Laurence couldn't help but be impressed by his astuteness, no doubt another result of his relationship with Charles.

"Very good." Alexander lowered his head enough to be cordial, then excused himself. "I shall be right back."

Prudence smiled as the boy made his way out of the dining room. "Oh, how *intriguing*."

"Quite," Abby said tightly, giving Charles and Grace a look. "But I suppose not altogether unexpected, since even he was told about a certain ladder he is far too young to know about."

"Why ever for?" Grace arched her eyebrows at Abby. "Mr. Wright built a lovely ladder so Maude and Blake might have their servants see to important castle improvements." She gave Abby a pointed look. "Namely, that a certain dangerous vine be removed before someone hurt themselves on it."

"Yet they did *not* remove it after we left, did they?" Abby said quickly and passionately enough to tell him just how much that vine meant to her.

"And if they did, Abigail?" he could not help but ask, giving her no choice but to look at him lest she be rude. "What harm would it do?" He winked. "If anything, I would think it cleared the way for a safe new beginning for future inhabitants interested in a late-night climb." When she narrowed her eyes at him, he merely shrugged. "Tell me I am wrong."

"You are wrong," Abby spat, suddenly caring nothing for good company. "That vine is harmless and should remain right where it is." Her cheeks grew rosy indeed as she nodded her head for good measure. "It *will* remain right where it is, for that matter."

"Will it, then?" He quirked the corner of his mouth, willing to talk in riddles all night if it meant her admitting the vine and Reginald were one and the same. Moreover, behind them. "When it is gone already, and the castle wall can once again breathe without its cloying, damaging, *overbearing* coverage."

"I have made a decision about part of our contract, Laurence," she said sharply, ripping away the witty banter. She looked from Charles back to him. "That is, if Lord Newcastle agrees to it."

When he glanced at Charles, the Englishman shrugged, clearly only willing to get so involved. Or so Laurence thought.

"And that is?" Laurence prompted Abby.

"That I finally step foot on a boat for the first time tomorrow, weather permitting, and visit that beautiful little island with a lighthouse just off the coast of this castle," she said. "That will fulfill our—"

"No." *The little minx.* He shook his head and frowned at her. "A bit of land off the coast of England is *not* what we agreed to."

"*Actually*—" she shrugged and shot him a triumphant upturn of her nose as she pointed out the loophole in their contract— "you specifically said, and I have the signed documentation to prove it, that I must travel anywhere with you that requires me stepping on a boat." She cocked her head at Charles. "Does it not take a boat to get to the lighthouse, Lord Newcastle?"

"It does," he said, bemused, before shrugging at Laurence. "Sorry, old chap."

He was about to respond when Alexander returned and handed Laurence a piece of driftwood as well as a small, sheathed blade. "Here you go, Mr. Wright."

Laurence glanced from the items to the boy. "What would you have me do with these?"

"I would have you prove that you are worthy to go into business with me once I am older and established." Alexander gestured at the wood. "And I task you to have it finished as soon as possible."

"All right." The boy meant business, so he kept his tone most serious. "And what would you ask of me?"

"As aforementioned that I would like to see evidence of your talent, I would have you carve that piece of wood into Aunt Abby," Alexander said, clearly surprising the lot of them based on the women's small gasps and the men's chuckles. "I hear you two are great friends, admirable friends, and I would like to see that in what you create."

How interesting a request. What did the boy know? Clearly enough that he knew Laurence had built a ladder.

"Why, Alexander?" he said. "Why do you want to see my friendship with your aunt carved in driftwood?"

"Because I want to see how skilled you are," Alexander said without preamble, perfectly logical. "And I feel the best way to do that is to see how you carve something meaningful." He smiled from Abby to Laurence. "And what is more meaningful than carving someone you care about? It certainly says more than carving a mere tree or a random face, does it not?"

It certainly did. How astute of the boy.

"You are quite right, good sir." He kept things businesslike because Alexander had earned that at the very least. "Though I must point out, building a ladder or even a ship is a considerably different task than what you ask of me. Both are skills but of a different nature."

"I do understand that." Alexander gestured at the piece of wood again. "Do you not see then, Mr. Wright?"

Apparently not. "Do enlighten me."

"The point of this exercise is less about your skill and more about your heart," he said quite astutely. "If you are above trying something that makes you uncomfortable, it says a lot about how far you are willing to go in business. Doing this proves you are at least willing to try new things."

"You understand business well, young Alexander," Laurence praised. "Because the most successful of us must be both adventurous and courageous." He allowed his gaze to linger on Abby not only because he liked the way she blushed, but because it was best to size up one's subject. Once he'd had a good eyeful, he looked at the boy again and nodded. "Challenge accepted. Might I prove myself worthy."

Alexander nodded with approval. "Might you indeed, Mr. Wright."

After that, the night resumed, and they enjoyed a lovely dinner which began with white soup, a rich combination of meat, cream, and almonds, followed by fish with wine and mushrooms, then lemon cheesecake.

Naturally, Abby continued engaging in conversation with anyone but him. While he did not like it because he enjoyed chatting with her, it made it easier to bid everyone goodnight early so he could work on his task. He would meet them over breakfast and looked forward to sailing—weather permitting—to the lighthouse tomorrow as Abby had moved that contractual task right along.

Grateful for the bottle of red wine and sweetmeats Harold had brought up along with a good surface to work on, Laurence unsheathed the blade, impressed with its sharpness. Then he poured a glass of wine, set the wood in front of him, and considered it. While he'd enjoyed woodcarving in all its various forms as a boy, it had been a long time since he had created anything beyond the confines of angles and measurements.

A long time since he'd let his mind roam beyond the tight confines his father had demanded of him. A realm beyond business and calculating his every move. A time when he could let every nuance of the wood take him rather than fight it within the walls of constricted dimensions.

"Constricted dimensions," he whispered, running his fingers over the wood. "Dimensions you do not possess, Abby. Not anymore."

He felt its curvatures and saw her face in them. Her body. How she had felt in his arms. The way her eyes had fluttered, and her lips fell apart in a breathless moan when he filled her.

"Yet this must be about friendship." Where to begin, though? "Here." He chipped off a small piece and set it aside, then eyed the larger piece. "And, of course, there."

Seeing it unfold in his mind, he ignored the wine and started with the larger piece seeing both so clearly now. Better put, he saw Abby clearly, indeed.

Chapter Fifteen

ABBY WAS CAUGHT unaware by the quick comradery Laurence had made with Charles and Alexander. Her brother-by-marriage, who still battled the Americans on occasion in his mind, had spent the greater part of the day holed up in his study with one. More surprising still, Eleanor claimed laughing could be heard as the day wore on. *Laughing.*

If all that were not enough, it seemed her nephew was somehow part of this big push her family appeared to be making that she be with Laurence. Because he built her a mere ladder and helped her climb down it.

She knew there was far more to it, but she was frustrated and felt cornered. This was her family, yet they seemed unable or unwilling to understand she refused to be with a man who forced her into anything. Someone who, if she did not give in, inevitably somehow went around her feelings. Something she thought he would stop doing after leaving her so abruptly after lovemaking.

Yet here he was at every turn ingratiating himself with her kin.

That told her he was starting his pursuit all over again. Perhaps coming at her from yet another angle. This one was by far the most effective, considering it included her family. Especially his conversation with Alexander earlier when her nephew had tasked him with carving her. She had never seen him interact with a child, and it warmed her traitorous heart.

She had thought a man like Laurence would be put off by a boy taking time away from the adult conversation, but he seemed the very opposite. If anything, based on how good he was with Alexander, it became painfully clear he would make a good father. An excellent one, at that.

"Dear *Lord*, Abby," Prudence said hours later as she and her sisters enjoyed glasses of claret and played cards. "What is keeping you down here when you clearly want to go see what Laurence is up to?" The corner of her mouth twitched with amusement. "Because he is clearly *up* for you."

Grace released a dainty snort. "How bold you have become since marrying Jacob, dear Prudence."

"And how dirty-minded you have become since marrying Charles," Prudence chastised, rounding her eyes at Grace before she looked at Abby most seriously. "Come, now, love. Why play these games?" She gestured at the door. "Why not go up there, see what he might be carving, and have a good, much-needed talk? Tell him everything you told us?"

"Because I will not risk it," she nearly said. "I will not chance that what Reginald warned me about might happen."

Instead, in no mood to keep fending off her sisters' well-meaning words, she bowed out of the game and begged them a good eve making it clear she was off to bed and nowhere else.

"We love you, sister," Grace called after her before she got too far.

"And look forward to your first—" Prudence tapped her finger against her lips—"I mean second, third—" she slid a saucy grin Abby's way and blew a kiss off her open palm—"I believe *fourth* adventure with our dashing Mr. Wright, tomorrow."

"I imagine you do," she muttered but could not help a small smile as she walked away from her sisters. They had both been down difficult roads with their previous husbands, so seeing them so happy now was good. Seeing them carefree in a way she hoped to be again someday.

Even though she would have been comfortable knocking on Laurence's door days ago to see how his project was coming along, they were nowhere near there now. So she rang for Eleanor to help her undress before it got too late, then stared out the window rather than stand on the balcony. The cold wind was more intense here than at MacLauchlin Castle, so she knew better than to go out at this hour.

Despite the beauty of clouds rushing by the moon over the sparkling sea, she inevitably found herself staring at the door connecting her room to Laurence's. Although obvious on Grace's part, knowing he was close was comforting. She might not be happy with him, but she liked having him nearby.

She drifted to his door and rested her hand on its surface for a moment before pressing her cheek against it, eager to hear what he was doing on the other side. There was only silence, though. Was he really carving her likeness as he saw it—in friendship? Taking that kind of time to prove to a boy that he was worthy of going into business with him someday?

Something she tried to learn more about when Eleanor helped prepare her for bed.

"Harold delivered Mr. Wright a bottle of wine and snacks, then was dismissed for the night," Eleanor revealed. "I know little more than that, my lady."

That was it and all she had to go on after Eleanor retired and Abby crawled into bed. She had never felt more conflicted and confused as she tried to sleep rather than imagine what he was doing. How he might see her in that driftwood.

Not surprisingly, that thought brought her back to how he had looked at her when they made love. The tenderness in his gaze as he ran his fingers along her jaw and down her neck. How he had trailed those same fingers so lightly between her breasts that her nipples had pebbled with awareness. With the pure thrill of being touched and worshiped like that.

"Because I *do* worship you, my love," he whispered in her ear, suddenly right there. He kissed her neck and ran his hand down her thigh, murmuring against the softness of her belly as he caressed the flesh between her thighs. "I adore every inch of you." He rubbed the tiny nub at the center of her pleasure. "I will never hurt you as Reginald did."

"Laurence," she gasped when he pressed but a mere finger inside her, and she let go only to open her eyes not to his mouth, traveling closer and closer to the juncture between her thighs but to daylight. She clenched the blanket by her side and bit back a groan as the peak she'd found in nothing more than a dream washed over her.

More than a little caught off guard that he had made her feel this way when asleep, she closed her eyes and waited for it to pass. Struggled to breathe even as her release continued ebbing through her, and all she could see was his face. Feel his touch.

Imagine that night together all over again.

Eventually, she drifted down, opened her eyes again, and looked at their adjoining door only to go still when she spied what sat on the desk beside it. Overwhelmed by emotion, she blinked to ensure she saw things straight before sitting up and covering her mouth.

What had Laurence done? *Created?*

She crawled out of bed and went to the delicate figurine that had once been nothing more than a piece of driftwood. Now it was…her. He had captured her face so perfectly there could be no doubt he had her features memorized. She bit back tears at her likeness breaking free of a vine wrapped around her over a balcony. At how joyous she seemed as she turned her face upward as though looking at the moon. As though seeing far beyond anything she dared dream.

"How very talented you are, Laurence," she murmured, amazed the flirtatious American who had been determined to lay with a trollop in a tavern was capable of *this* beautifully crafted object. Her gaze fell to the little piece beside the figurine, and she pressed her lips together. More tears escaped as she picked up the delicate wooden pendant attached to a silk ribbon. Caught within a circle, two tiny figures stood on a balcony beside each other. A balcony free of vines and ladders just as she and Laurence had stood on the balcony of her new room at MacLauchlin Castle.

Free of everything that had brought them to that point.

Yet still, despite so much beauty and heartfelt emotion, Reginald got through.

"If ever I pass and another man tries to make you his, you will see it, my Abby." He had looked at her with concern from a chair he could never escape from. *"Like my beloved daughter, you will see it in grand gestures and tokens of appreciation. It will all seem so incredibly romantic until it is not."*

It did seem that, indeed. So incredibly touching and romantic that she did not hear the rap on her door until Eleanor stuck her head in and smiled. "Good morning, my lady."

"Good morning." She looked from the figurine to Eleanor and perked a brow. "Might you know how this arrived in my room when I was sleeping?"

Eleanor's mouth dropped as she joined Abby. "No, my lady." She marveled at the figurine. "But how stunning." Her gaze widened even further, and she put a hand to her heart when she spied the piece resting in Abby's open palm. "Goodness, Mr. Wright is very talented, is he not?"

"He is, in more ways than one, considering my doors are supposed to be locked." Wondering if her maid was somehow involved, she narrowed her eyes at the key on her desk. "Yet you managed to walk right in." She tried not to grow overheated at the thought Laurence might have been there when she dreamt of him. "So, how did Mr. Wright get in?"

"Likely the same way I did, my lady." Eleanor flinched and put said key into the door she had just entered, only for it to go around without clicking. "While Lord and Lady Newcastle provided you and Mr. Wright rooms that have been renovated, it seems the old doors and their locks have not been replaced and are quite useless."

"But of course, they are," she muttered, cursing Grace. "And,

I am sure, not destined to be replaced while we are here?"

Because why stop midnight trysts?

Eleanor shrugged and offered an excited smile, obviously having no answer. "The weather is pleasant, and everyone is already downstairs having breakfast. Might we prepare you to join them before such a big day?"

She frowned. "What time is it?"

"Later than you usually sleep, my lady," Eleanor confessed. "But still quite enough time to sail and enjoy a pleasant afternoon."

"I suppose it must be," she murmured.

"Are you not excited?" Eleanor gushed, pulling appropriate clothing out of Abby's armoire. "Lord Newcastle says it should be a nice day for boating."

"Splendid." While she had come up with the quickly hatched idea to avoid a long trip with Laurence, she could admit to feeling a mix of emotions because she *had* wanted to travel to a new country with him. Yet, when he'd grown so smug last night comparing Reginald to the vine and thinking he had the whole situation figured out, she had grown most frustrated. Therefore, the lighthouse became the perfect opportunity to rip away any hold he thought he'd had over her.

Now? She glanced at what he had carved. Perhaps there was a little less to be upset with him about, even if Reginald would have said otherwise.

"There is one other thing of relevance, my lady," Eleanor said softly as if she did not want to be overheard. "Although I should not gossip."

"Yet you will." She also lowered her voice to make sure her maid felt everything properly hush-hushed. "So, do tell?"

"Well." Eleanor looked left and right as though they were standing in a room full of people, and she wanted to be discreet. "According to rumor—"

"You mean, according to Harold." Abby smiled, sure to make her maid feel completely at ease, so she confessed every last tidbit.

"Quite right, my lady," Eleanor admitted, clearly more eager to gossip than worry over revealing her source.

"And that is?" Abby prompted when she took even a second too long to respond.

"He was up *all* night." Eleanor's eyes went round as saucers. "Mr. Wright never slept but spent his entire evening carving your figurine for you." With a pitter-patter flourish of her hand against her chest and a most notable swoon-worthy flicker in her eyes, she shook her head. "Harold tried to come in several times lest your love needed anything, but he was sent away abruptly, for Mr. Wright's depiction of you, my lady, would *not* be interrupted. Simple as that. He was *quite* firm and gallant about it."

All night? Seriously? And good God, even her *maid* had figured out Abby had fallen in love with Laurence? That was alarming indeed. Abby refrained from looking skyward at Eleanor's dramatic take on things but thanked her for the information and focused on getting ready. More so, she did her best not to overthink Laurence's actions. His remarkably touching gesture. Instead, she dressed warmly and headed downstairs with his pendant and figurine in a satchel to give to either him or Alexander when the time was right.

"Good morning," Prudence said gaily when she joined them. Ever the morning person, no matter how late she went to sleep, her sister smiled at her. "How did you sleep?"

"Quite well, thank you." Having no choice but to sit beside Laurence, she smiled at Charles and Grace. "Thank you for such a beautiful room and view."

"But of course." Grace met her smile. "We are so glad you liked it. Suspected you might."

There were no thinly disguised glances of amusement that her sisters or their husbands knew about the figurine and pendant she had awoken to. All were a-chatter about the day's events.

"We shall set out straight away after breakfast," Charles said, "then spend the afternoon and evening enjoying the island. I have to see to a few things out there, so the timing is perfect."

"So, we are spending the night, then?" Abby asked, surprised. She thanked a servant when he set down a plate of eggs, freshly baked brioche bread, and a cup of tea in front of her.

"Yes, if it would not be too much trouble?" Charles glanced from Grace to Abby. "Your sister thought you would enjoy seeing the lighthouse lit up and perhaps get a feel for being surrounded by the sea overnight for any future adventures that might take you a tad farther out."

"How forward-thinking of her." She narrowed her eyes ever so slightly at Grace before turning her attention back to Charles. "That sounds lovely, but are there places to sleep?"

"There are," he said. "We have lodgings for the lighthouse keepers and a few cottages for visitors. I fear they are a bit rustic, but an experience to be sure."

"I have already taken the liberty of having one of my maids let Miss Eleanor know to pack your overnight belongings." Grace's eyes twinkled. "So *do* say you are on board, Abby."

"Of course I am." And would have been more excited if she and Laurence were not at odds. She smiled at everyone but avoided eye contact with him because, quite frankly, she was afraid of what she might feel if she looked into his eyes.

She was, however, fully aware of his presence beside her when she glanced at him every so often. He was not dressed in his usual clothing but much like a fisherman in trousers rather than breeches. In addition, he wore a dark blue sweater that might have lent him an unkempt look, but combined with how well the color accentuated his eyes and a light layer of stubble on his jaw, made him that much more attractive. As alluring as he'd been the night when he'd dressed plainly in their tavern.

While she pretended to inhale the scent of her tea, she instead drew in his spicy masculine scent. An addictive mix of cedar, pine, and fresh air. Somehow, it matched the man who had carved that figurine for her. Who had seen her in a light even she did not. Who saw not just a whole new type of beauty within her but incredible courage.

"Well then," Charles said, smiling at the lot of them when they finished eating. "Are we ready to go, family?"

"We are," Alexander said tentatively. "Although I had rather hoped..."

"Hoped what?" Grace prompted when he trailed off.

When Alexander seemed hesitant, Charles prompted him as well. "What is it, son?"

Alexander glanced Laurence's way. "Well, I was hoping to see how Mr. Wright's project is progressing."

Almost as if Laurence waited for her to speak up before he replied, silence fell for a moment before he gave Alexander an apologetic look. "Well, these things take time and—"

"No," she blurted, speaking before thinking, but this was again what Reginald had warned her about. How swiftly men could fib, no matter to whom. "Mr. Wright completed his task." Refraining from sharing the pendant, she fished the figurine out of her satchel and set it on the table. "And it is quite—" she cleared her throat when it thickened with emotion—"lovely."

Her sisters gasped, and Alexander's eyes went wide.

"That is *quite* the piece, Mr. Wright." Her nephew's impressed gaze went from it to Laurence. "Did you truly create that, for I have never seen anything so spectacular."

"Alexander." Charles shook his head. "You know better."

"Indeed, I do, and my apologies, Mr. Wright," Alexander said readily enough, looking Laurence in the eyes before he resumed admiring the piece every bit as much as the rest of them. "I must say you very much met my criteria for doing business with someday." He grew quite businesslike and nodded once before he seemed to catch himself and set things straight. "Though, if I were to be honest, I would have preferred you presented this to me personally."

"And I appreciate you would have preferred that, young Alexander." Laurence sipped his tea, set the cup down, and looked the lad in the eyes, not coddling him in the least but firm rather than condescending. "Yet you never stipulated that in our arrangement, did you?" He cocked his head and thought about it. "If I recall correctly, you wanted a representation of your Aunt Abby, of which I, one way or another, provided as soon as possible, which means, essentially, whenever it suited me. You never stipulated any additional details."

Laurence clearly let him think about that and did not mince words. "In the future, when making a deal, I suggest you be more direct." He shook his head, standing by what was clearly his tried-and-true business method. "Be it friend, family, foe, or stranger, never depend on a handshake or word of mouth but a signed contract with witnesses. A legal contract drawn up by a lawyer is always best. Something you can fall back on that no one can doubt."

Straight to the point, when the boy hesitated, he let Alexander know where he went wrong.

"Moreover, when making a deal, clarify every aspect. What, why, when, where, and by whom," he said. "Otherwise, you might not get your product from the person you thought, or where or when you needed it by. That, in turn, means you will not be able to provide for your clientele in a timely manner." He gave Alexander a warning look. "If that happens, you lose said clientele and, very likely, your business too."

By the time he was finished, Alexander was not offended in the least but clearly quite enamored. In addition, he was obviously resolved to do things right next time because he and Laurence kept talking about it after they left the dining room, and everyone bundled up for the trip.

"That is some wood carving," Grace said softly after they put on winter coats. "There are no words."

"Oh, but there very much are," Prudence corrected, her gaze most serious when she looked at Abby. "And if you are too foolish to see it at this point, then shame on you."

"Sister," Grace chastised.

"What?" Prudence frowned at Grace. "If ever true love existed, it is in that carving." Ever the valiant protector of love nowadays, she yanked on a warm winter cap and narrowed her eyes at Abby. "I have never seen anything so beautiful besides you, yourself, and can only imagine the thoughts Laurence had while carving it." She shook her head sharply. "You would be a fool to turn him away, sister. An absolute fool."

When Abby looked Grace's way, her gentler sister offered no softer words. "I agree with her entirely, darling." She glanced from Laurence, who stood talking with the men by the door, back to Abby. "There was no doubt in my mind when you arrived yesterday that he is madly in love with you, and goodness, that figurine more than proves it."

Unsure how to respond, she kept quiet as they piled into the carriage and set out. Yet she was never more aware of Laurence, whom, yet again, she had no choice but to sit beside. Rather than a proper gentleman's coat and hat, he wore a sturdy wool jacket and the knit cap of a fisherman. Common looks that, once again, she found overwhelmingly attractive. Likely because he seemed more at ease in that attire than anything he had worn thus far.

Less like a ridiculously wealthy heir and more like…him.

She startled at the thought, but it felt right. Laurence might have inherited a great deal of wealth and certainly knew how to make his own money, but the man who sat beside her now was the real him. As was the figurine he had carved for her. Not wealth and pomp but a man who could find genuine contentment as a carpenter or indeed, whatever job caught his fancy.

What to make of that? What to make of all the diversity he suddenly threw at her? A persona Reginald would have never spared a second look at, so perhaps fell beyond the spectrum of aristocratic men she should not trust?

It was not long before they arrived at Charles' sailboat. While not overly large, it was clearly well-built with a single mast and an encased area for the captain and a few passengers. When they arrived at the ramp going up to the starboard side of the boat, Laurence held out his hand to her. "Are you ready then, Abigail?"

His gaze never left her face. He never took his eyes off her for a moment. "For this fulfills the first part of our contract."

No, I am not ready. How could I be when you are the kind of man I was warned about, yet not like him at all? How can I be when you are Reginald's villain and my hero?

Even so, she was getting ready to step foot on a boat for the first time, so she had a decision to make. Would she take the villain's—or the hero's—hand?

Chapter Sixteen

W HILE IRRITATED ABBY had chosen a little island with a lighthouse off the coast of England as her grand adventure on a boat, Laurence could not be more pleased by the flustered look in her eyes when she'd joined everyone downstairs earlier. The way pink dusted had her cheekbones when she glanced at him every so often.

She might not have spoken to it, but he knew she liked what he had carved for her. Saw it in the way her gaze softened on the figurine when she did not think he was looking. What had she done with the pendant, he wondered, because she hadn't set it out nor mentioned it? He could only hope she liked it. Hoped she understood when she looked at it that he always wanted them to stand on a new balcony together.

To stand as one as they began adventure upon an adventure together.

That said, he made a point of being the one who helped her onto Charles's boat because he wanted, no, *needed*, to see her expression. And how very worth it, it was, from how her hand tightened in his to how her gaze sparkled with excitement. Her eyes, impossibly green in this lighting, rounded, and a smile blossomed when the boat swayed underfoot.

"I have to help Charles and Jacob see to the rigging and set sail," he said. "So perhaps you would like to join your sisters and take cover for now?"

"I would really rather not." Evidently willing to talk to him now, her wide-eyed gaze darted everywhere as though she could not take in everything fast enough. "If I will not be in the way, I would very much like to remain on deck."

"Of course." He smiled and urged her to hold the railing, grateful she wore sturdy shoes. "Be sure to hold on until you have adjusted to the sway of the boat. Better said, until you get your sea legs."

She nodded. "Of course."

Fortunately, the day was perfect for sailing, and they set out smoothly. He could not help but smile again at Abby's response when the wind filled the sail, and the boat lurched forward. She squealed with delight and laughed, her cheeks rosy with excitement.

"If I did not know better—" he said when he rejoined her and noticed how well she maintained her balance—"I would say you are a natural-born sailor."

"Standing on a boat does take some getting used to," she admitted, grinning. "But it is not as difficult as one might think."

"Not on such a calm sea," he agreed, chuckling. "It can be tricky, however, on rougher waters."

"I can imagine." She peered over the edge and took in the glittering sea and minuscule waves. "I have heard waves can get quite high. How much can a boat handle?"

"It depends on the size of the vessel," he said. "And waves *can* get high. High enough, even the largest ship cannot climb them."

"Oh, dear." She looked at him warily. "That must be terrifying."

"I would imagine." He kept things vague less she grew frightened. "That is why a good captain and crew are recommended. Sailors who understand the skies and how weather can affect the water."

"Yet even they must be susceptible to unexpected storms," Abby deduced, watching him closely. "Ones they cannot outrun."

"They have been," he admitted. "But the outcome far outweighs the risk when it comes to business and, more so these days, pleasure. We are in a day and age where more and more people travel. Steamboats are already in use commercially, so I imagine it is only a matter of time before they transport passengers." He could just imagine it. Hoped it came to pass in their lifetime. "Mark my words, the day will come when we can cross the world in half the time. When invention upon invention speeds everything up indeed."

"You are quite the dreamer."

"I prefer the term 'visionary,' but yes, in part, a dreamer too, I suppose." He could not help but look at her with hope because his words very much had a double innuendo. "As should everyone be to a degree, for how else will we see the future we are so determined to create?"

Clearly catching it, her gaze lingered on his face for a moment before she stared at the sea again and spoke a tad more softly. "Thank you for the figurine, Laurence. It is…quite lovely. Beautiful, actually."

"It but mirrors its inspiration." He could not help but push back a curl that blew in her eyes. "And what of the pendant? I noticed you did not share it."

"Very touching," she said softly. "Again, thank you."

It might be the sting of the wind, but he swore she blinked back tears before she gathered herself and looked at him rather hesitantly. "So I must assume you snuck into my room last night, for I cannot see your valet having been so inappropriate."

"I did." And he had never seen anything so beautiful as Abby sleeping with her shimmering red hair fanned out around her. She'd been murmuring and smiling in her sleep as if having a splendid dream. "I felt the pieces I carved rather personal, so I wanted you to see them first. Wanted you to decide whether or not to share them with anyone else."

"And if I had decided against it?" she wondered. "What would you have told Alexander?"

"The truth," he replied. "Then I would have requested a second chance and another piece of driftwood."

"Yet you were getting ready to lie to him when he asked about it this morning."

"Only because I wanted to give you time," he said. "Though I must confess I was glad you did not need it."

"Why?"

"Truly?"

"I would not have asked otherwise."

"Because sharing your figurine seemed to be another step in your letting go of the past." He wanted to cup her cheek and feel her soft skin but refrained. "Letting go by sharing with others how far you have come considering you have, indeed, broken free of that balcony and vine."

"I see," she said softly, turning her face to the sea again.

Did she? He could only hope based on the resolution in her eyes. A sense of newly found peace if he did not know better. Either way, he wanted Abby's mind on the here and now for her first boat ride, so he focused on giving her the best experience possible.

"Come." He took her hand. "You must see the view from the stern."

Abby yet again proved as she made her way along that she maneuvered a boat well. So well, he suspected she would do just fine on rougher waters.

"Oh, how lovely." Her eyes lit up as she took in the magnificent cliff-ridden coastline and Charles and Grace's castle from afar. "I always wondered what it might be like to see land from water." Her voice dropped an octave. "To watch it finally fade away into the distance."

He could tell by the sadness that flashed in her gaze she had imagined it one time too many.

"It can be as gratifying as arriving at your final destination," he said, hoping she caught the double innuendo in that too.

Although tempted to talk more, most especially about the

night they had made love and he left her bedroom, he did not want to take from the moment. So they settled into a comfortable silence for a time and enjoyed the view before he gestured in Charles's direction. "The winds are in our favor, so it won't be long before we reach the lighthouse. Perhaps you would like to take the helm if Lord Newcastle agrees?"

"Surely not." Her eyes rounded again. "You mean, steer the boat?"

"That is precisely what I mean." He could not help but wink. "You know how I am about you taking control of your own adventures."

Even though her cheeks grew rosier still, and she, without a doubt, remembered when he'd urged her to take control prior to lovemaking, she cocked her head. "Do you really think he would let me?"

"It cannot hurt to ask." He took her hand again and led her up to where Charles stood manning the wheel. The lighthouse had grown considerably closer, but there was still time. "I have a favor to ask, my lord." When Charles perked his brows in question, Laurence grinned. "It seems Lady Somerset would like to take the wheel."

"Would she?" Charles met his grin and eyed Abby with amusement. "So soon? You have only just set sail for the first time."

"If you would not mind." Abby eyed the large wooden wheel with anticipation. "I think I rather might."

"Then, by all means." He handed the wheel off to Laurence first. "I shall leave you to it."

"I will help you get the feel of it, then let you take the helm." Seeing a prime opportunity to get closer to her, he urged Abby to grab the wheel on either side, then stood behind her and rested his hands over hers. Then, bringing his mouth close enough to her ear that she could feel the warmth of his breath, he told her how things should go. "You need but keep the wheel straight and aim for the lighthouse. On a day like today, you will feel very little tug in either direction, yet it is there." He inhaled the sweet scent of her hair and loosened his hold over her hands just enough. "Do you feel that, Abigail? Do you feel how much control you actually have?"

"I do because there is *indeed* a slight pull to the right," she said breathlessly enough to let him know more than steering the boat was having an effect on her. "It is quite the thing, is it not? Being in control of so very much?"

"It is." He kept his hands rested loosely over hers. "Now try giving in to the pull so you might experience what the boat does. It will give you a better feel for steering. Then, when you are ready, return to the course that will bring you to where you want to go." He so wanted to drop a kiss on the side of her delicate neck and feel the warmth of her skin beneath his lips. "Because whatever happens in life, however many side adventures you take, there is always a welcome port at the end waiting for you."

"Why do I get the feeling we are no longer talking about boats?" she murmured, turning her head just enough to put her lips closer to his.

"Because we are not," he said. "Not entirely." He squeezed her hands briefly. "Are you ready to try, then?"

"I am." She nodded and looked ahead again. "Very much so."

"Are you sure because I am going to remove my hands altogether?"

"I am sure."

"Excellent." He removed his hands and smiled when she made a little sound of pleasure and let the wheel slip right and, with it, turned the boat a scant fraction before she gently steered it back toward the island.

"Very good," he praised. Unable to help himself, he dropped a kiss on her cheek and stood beside her rather than behind her. "Very good indeed."

"It rather is, isn't it?" Abby was positively aglow and quite confident as she smiled from him to the sea ahead. "What a *wonderful* feeling!"

"Well done, sister," Prudence exclaimed from the deck. She shaded her hand against the sun and smiled up at Abby. "Captaining a boat well suits you."

"Yes, it does," Grace agreed, grinning.

"The currents around the island can be a tad tricky," Charles said to Laurence, smiling as well from beside his wife. "Would you rather I take her into port?"

"God no, friend." He smiled at Abby. "With my help, Lady Somerset will bring her in just fine."

"Surely *not*." Abby's eyes widened on the tiny island, and she shook her head. "I could not *possibly*."

"You can and will." He stood behind her again and rested his hands on her shoulders. "I will be here every step of the way, love. I will not let things go astray."

"Then why do I feel so uncertain?" Her voice was a little shaky, and her words were as full of double meaning as he had been.

"Because you have not learned to fully trust me yet." He leaned close to her ear again. "But you will, Abigail. I promise you that."

She offered no response other than a little shiver he knew had to do with her awareness of his proximity rather than an actual chill.

"The closer we get to the island, the better you will get an idea of the current's direction." He rested his hands over hers again. "If the wheel tugs to the right, that is the direction of your current. Left then that is the direction. If there is no tug, it is straight in or out."

"And how can you tell which? Straight in or out?"

"By the speed of your approach." He pointed at the dock in the distance. "Because the current is taking us to the right, it is best to align to the left of the dock. As the sail lowers, the boat will slow considerably, and we will drift until we dock accordingly. Had this been a larger ship, oarsmen would be involved."

She frowned at him over her shoulder. "How do you know

how far left?"

"Let's just say it's something you get a better sense of the more you do it." It took everything in him not to close his mouth over hers. To taste the sea on her warm, plush lips, tear away her hat, and let her hair down. See her long, wild locks blowing in the wind. "You seem to excel at everything you do, so I imagine it will only be a matter of time before you master this."

However unintentional the act, when her dainty tongue wet her lips, he about groaned and pulled her into his arms, their audience be damned. He had never wanted a woman so fiercely. Knew he never would again. When their gazes caught and her pupils flared, he knew she understood just how aroused she made him.

"It is nearly that time," he murmured, wishing to hell they were in bed, and he referred to something else. Yet, alas, he heard the sail being lowered. "Are you ready to steer a boat ashore for the first time, Abigail?"

"I suppose I must be," she said hoarsely before she looked forward again. "So, steer a tad to the left?"

"Yes," he confirmed. "I will adjust accordingly as needed."

And so, Abby did as recommended, rather shocking him with how well she maneuvered them in. He hardly had to adjust her steering before they sailed up slowly and quite smoothly alongside the dock.

"Well done, sister," Prudence exclaimed, beaming up at her.

"Indeed." Grace smiled just as widely. "You are a natural."

Alexander grinned, quite impressed. "You very much are, Aunt Abby."

"I did it," Abby exclaimed as Jacob and Charles tied off. "I docked a boat!"

When her eyes rounded on Laurence, and her triumphant, overjoyed smile made everything inside him light up, he became acutely aware of how hard he had fallen for her. More to the point, it made him overly aware of just how heartbreaking it would be if she turned him away in the end.

"You *did* dock a boat." He smiled in return. "And did so very well, Abigail."

"Abby," she softly. "You taught me how to steer a boat, so I imagine we should be back on a more friendly first-name sort of basis again."

More progress, still. His heart soared. "Very well, Abby." He could not seem to pull his gaze from her eyes. Look anywhere but into their emerald depths. "I *am* sorry, you know. Sorry for pushing you when I should not have."

She considered him for a moment and was about to reply when Prudence called up. "Are you two coming, or do you intend to spend the night *here?*"

The thought had crossed his mind. To hell with the cold weather; he would wrap Abby up in his arms and keep her warm until the end of time.

"We are coming." Abby smiled from Prudence to the towering lighthouse in anticipation. "Very much coming."

As it turned out, there were two very surprised lighthouse keepers who were delighted they were visiting. Charles introduced them as Hugh and Daniel. Both were heavily bearded and weatherworn. Hugh had salt and pepper hair, and Daniel's was pure white. Seamen to the bone, they welcomed them into a cozy room a few flights up in the lighthouse where the men ate and kept themselves entertained when not maintaining the light and cottages.

"How charming." Abby admired the room with its plush old couches, rather ancient-looking wooden chairs, and the crackling fire with a pot hanging over it. Rusty lanterns hung here and there, and heavily melted candles sat on a wooden dining table. They were up high enough to enjoy a pleasant view of the sea. "Rustic, indeed."

"I thought so, too." Grace smiled warmly at the overseers. "I hope you do not mind us popping over? We thought we might spend the night."

"Mind?" Daniel chuckled and patted his portly stomach, his

genuine cockney accent putting Abby's precarious attempt at the tavern to shame. "Not at all. The more, the merrier. It is a fine day for fishin' and fillin' our bellies." He issued a rather sloppy bow and winked at Alexander while pointing upward. "Then may'ap we will see if we can light a few lamps up top this evenin'."

Alexander smiled. "That sounds most delightful, Sir Daniel."

"It does," Abby exclaimed, smiling wider still. "Might I join you?"

"Well, of course, my lady." Hugh bowed from the waist with a telling sparkle of appreciation in his eyes. Likely somewhere in his early forties and rather fit, he was clearly taken by her. "I will show you personally if you would allow me?"

While tempted to tell the bloke she was spoken for, she was not. Nor was that the way to go about things.

"I would like that, Hugh." Abby smiled winningly before glancing from Laurence to Hugh. "As long as you do not mind my dear friend, Laurence joining us? I fear we have become quite inseparable of late."

Had they then? How very nice to hear.

"Of course not, my lady." Not bothering to glance Laurence's way, Hugh's smile only broadened, his confidence admirable. "As Daniel said, the more, the merrier."

"Indeed." Prudence steered the conversation back to everyone else. "As I would like to go as well." She glanced at Jacob. "And perhaps my husband?"

"Naturally." Jacob looked at her affectionately. "Where you go, I follow, my love."

"Well then, it will be a royal night in the ole' ligh'house, to be sure." Daniel chuckled and rubbed his hands in anticipation, then grabbed a piece of wood off a small pile and tossed it on the fire. "It's bound to be a cold one, so let us see to 'fings before the sun goes down and our tower lights up."

"Very good." Charles nodded in agreement. "We brought extra provisions to help hold you over until the next time you go to the mainland as well as a few baskets of food prepared by our kitchen for everyone to enjoy tonight."

Daniel offered a crooked grin. "Any chance you brought some of your fine Sco'ish whisky, my lord?"

Acting very much *among the people* rather than an aristocrat, Charles also issued a tilt of the corner of his mouth. "But, of course, my friend."

"Good man." Daniel clasped Charles's shoulder and chuckled. "Then a *fine* night it shall be!"

Undoubtedly, it would be based on the way Abby was already quite animated as she and Alexander strolled about the room engaged in conversation. Not surprisingly, the boy was educated about his surroundings, from the lighthouse itself to the battles and shipwrecks that had happened beyond its walls. Abby, in turn, seemed riveted by anything and everything she could learn.

When the women set to making tea soon thereafter, Laurence and the men headed back to the ship to unload the provisions they had brought. In the brief time they had been inside, the winds had kicked up, and clouds darkened the horizon.

"It might be you, and yours are 'ere for longer than expected." Daniel eyed the clouds as only a seaman could. "Per'aps a day longer if I read that storm correctly."

"An extra day or two will not hurt anything," Charles assured Jacob when he glanced at him with concern. "The nursemaid will care well for Cecelia in our absence. Besides, I think it will do the sisters good to enjoy an adventure together." He shrugged and shot Laurence a knowing look. "Especially Abby, as she is very much the adventuresome sort, my friend."

"Indeed." Jacob chuckled. "I do believe before all is said and done, you will have to build Abby her own ship, Laurence, or else she might sail away with yours."

"And she may have it if she wants." The idea of her sailing her own ship made him proud. "Though I would rather build one for her to her specifications."

"You are a match made in heaven." Charles clasped his

shoulder and laughed. "Truly meant for one another." He shook his head. "Most chaps would be appalled at the idea of a woman sailing her own ship, but not you, it seems."

"Why would I be?" He gave them a pointed look. "It is well known a woman or two captained her own ship during the golden age of piracy, so why not now?"

"I could not agree more," Hugh agreed, tossing in his two-pence with a tad too much relish. "I think Abby, I mean Lady Somerset, would look quite the sight sailing her own ship. Bloody impressive, at that."

"I imagine she will, old chap." Jacob made things clear as he saw them. "As my friend Laurence's wife."

"Indeed." Charles tossed Hugh a warning look and supported the union as well. "With any luck, soon to be my new brother-by-marriage."

Where some might have thought a duke's word held more sway than an earl's, it was clear Charles had the final say in these parts. Not because he was this lighthouse and its overseer's lord either, but because he was very much one of them. His title meant nothing to Hugh, but his history as a seaman clearly did because he nodded once and mumbled what sounded like an *if you say so, cap'n.*

Laurence was not concerned about Hugh. Not now that Abby had made it clear all was not lost between the two of them. Nor, if he had his say, would it ever be. If the lighthouse man kept pursuing her despite being warned, he would step in as he knew how to fight hand to fist but did not see it coming to that.

Rather, he banked on things going another way entirely.

Chapter Seventeen

ABBY COULD NOT decide which part of her day had been the most splendid because every aspect had been incredibly wonderful. From the moment Laurence had taken her hand, and she'd stepped onto a sailboat for the first time, to this very moment standing beside him on the balcony at the top of the lighthouse while the lanterns were being lit.

It felt like a dream come true.

Her sisters had already claimed it far too cold the moment they arrived and returned downstairs, leaving her alone with Laurence.

"This is *incredible*." Pulling her collar more tightly around her neck as the icy wind gusted and lightning flashed over the turbulent sea, she smiled at Laurence, who did his best to protect her from the brunt of the wind. "I am quite sure I have *never* felt so alive."

While she might say such, that was by no means true. Steering Charles's sailboat with Laurence at her back had been every bit as enthralling. The thrill of the open sea, combined with the desire he'd invoked, had been intoxicating. Untouchable. Worth doing a thousand times over. Then, of course, there was the feeling of making love to him. Because nothing had ever made her feel more alive than that, and she imagined nothing ever would.

When she'd taken his hand earlier and stepped into the boat, she had decided to treat him as her hero rather than her enemy, as Reginald would have insisted. While she and Laurence certainly needed to talk, her sisters were right about her American, and she saw it clearly in the figurine he had carved for her. In the pendant he had so painstakingly created.

It was time to push past the fear her late husband had instilled in her and try to trust Laurence.

"Just wait until you see what comes next," Laurence said, pulling her back to the present.

When she shivered, he pulled off his coat and wrapped it around her shoulders while continuing to take the main force of the wind.

"I think what you soon see will make you feel more alive still," he went on. "You need but face the sea in any direction."

"Put this back on." She frowned and tried to remove his coat, but he stopped her and shook his head. "I'm used to this weather, love. Keep it."

Even though she should contradict him referring to her more and more as *love*, it was impossible to push the denial past her lips. She could, however, prevent him from freezing to death. So, she buttoned his jacket over hers, nudged him aside, gripped the chilly railing with her gloved hands, and made things clear. "If you are determined to wear so little, then stand behind me so I might take the brunt of the wind." When he went to deny her, she shook her head sharply and frowned. "Do it, or we shall be right back where we started."

The corner of his mouth shot up, and a dimple erupted in his cheek. "If that means we are right back in the tavern, then so be it."

"Laurence," she warned, not taking no for an answer. "Behind me."

His mouth inched up even higher, and the devil lit his eyes. "I suppose I could be asked worse things of such a beautiful woman."

Her cheeks warmed at the compliment. More so, still, the way he looked at her when he said it. "Indeed, you could."

She tried to say more, something witty, but could not find her voice when he stepped behind her, wrapped his arms around her, and murmured in her ear that body heat was the best way to warm one's self. As she had on the boat, she became solely aware of him now. His hard body against hers. The way his hot breath fanned her neck. How it felt like pure sinful fire rolled over her skin until it pooled between her thighs.

"Now watch," he said softly. "It will happen at any moment now."

No sooner did he say it than newly lit lanterns caught the concave mirrors above, and beautiful bright light burst out in every direction, igniting the white-tipped waves. It was like standing at the spectacular epicenter of a glorious star exploding. As if she were at the center of God's light shining down on the world.

"This is…" she whispered and shook her head. "There are no words."

"No." His voice sounded hoarser than before as he wrapped his arms more firmly around her. "There are not."

As the two of them had been on the boat when watching the English shore fade into the distance, they fell into a comfortable silence. One that felt just as kindred somehow as talking endlessly with one another. It most certainly did not hurt that she was wrapped up in his scent and warmth, either.

"Once again, I find the need to thank you, Laurence," she said softly, leaning her head back against his chest. "Thank you for all of this. Every last bit."

"You can thank your sisters for this," he said, his voice a deep rumble against her back, making her all that much more aware of him. "It might have been your idea to come here, but I imagine it was your sisters' idea that we stay overnight."

"Ah, yes." She nearly rolled her eyes. "Hence our convenient lack of sleeping arrangements."

As it turned out, there were only two small cottages outside of the lighthouse keepers' quarters which included an extra room. Grace had made crystal clear she, Charles, and Alexander would stay in the lighthouse and everyone else in the cottages. Naturally, Prudence had made it equally clear she would not be sharing a cottage with Abby but with her own husband.

So, well executed, she and Laurence had no choice but to share a cottage.

"I would not say we have a *lack* of sleeping arrangements," Laurence said, amusement in his voice. "If anything, I would say we are most well off."

"Be that as it may." Abby wiggled until she could turn in his arms and look him in the eyes. "We are not nearly where you think we are yet, Laurence. I do hope you understand that?"

"I do," he said obediently, yet that same twinkle from earlier was there. A look that told her he had her very much where he wanted her. "We shall do nothing but sleep."

She meant to slip away from what had turned into an intimate position but felt caught in his gaze. In the way he took her in. How he adored her with his eyes in a way other men could not. Goodness knows men had flirted and looked at her with desire, but somehow it all meant so much more when Laurence did it. Not just to her, but to him. He had a way of seeing beyond her physical appearance to what was inside.

A way of seeing something in her that she suspected even she could not fully see.

"Better still, perhaps we will talk about things that need talking about?" she said so softly her words nearly vanished on the wind. "I do believe it past time we do that, yes?"

"Yes." His hand was surprisingly warm when he cupped her cheek. "I would like nothing more, Abby. You cannot know how much I mean that."

If the figurine he had sculpted of her was anything to go on, she very much could. More than that, she felt the same. Felt it so strongly she leaned into his touch and closed her eyes. Abby wanted to feel more of this, *him*, and she would have said so if his mouth had not closed over hers first.

She should have pulled away and waited until after they'd talked, but that would have been equivalent to her saying "no" to climbing down a ladder. Standing on a high balcony. Stepping foot on a boat. Steering that same boat into port. Especially when his kiss beat all those things by far.

And what a kiss it was.

One that told her no matter what, he would never give up on her. Never quit trying.

Quick to passion, he folded her in his arms, pulled her against him more tightly still, and somehow kissed her more deeply than he ever had before. So deeply, the thunder rumbling overhead and the plump, icy raindrops suddenly falling faded into the background.

All that existed was him and the warmth that filled her when in his embrace.

In fact, they might have stayed there all night through the incoming storm had Daniel not laughed and bellowed down from above where he had been lighting the lanterns. "All right then, lovelies, you have had your fill of my light'ouse's glory. Time to come down and enjoy a wee dram, good food, and even better company."

She smiled against Laurence's lips and pulled back slightly to say, "Somehow, I think if we say no, he will throw us over his shoulders and make it happen regardless."

Laurence returned her smile. "He *does* seem driven that way."

She ran her fingers along his stubbled jaw. "So I suppose we must."

"Indeed," he murmured, brushing his lips across hers one last time before they reluctantly headed back downstairs.

Truth be told, as much as she had wanted to make their great escape now, she ended up enjoying the evening and was glad they stayed. The freshly caught seasoned cod and pickled vegetables were delicious, and the company wonderful. Alexander stayed on for a while before he went to bed, then she and her sisters had a grand time, as did their husbands.

It seemed out on their tiny island, free of civilization, everyone could just be who they were. Not titled lords and ladies but people who did not need to put on airs and enjoy one another's company. While Hugh clearly enjoyed looking at her, he was noticeably cautious about being flirtatious. Meanwhile, she skipped claret and sampled her first serving of Scottish whisky.

Then another glass still when Daniel pulled out his fiddle and started playing.

After that, as the storm raged outside, and under strict agreement, no waltzing would be involved, Hugh taught them steps that had never made it into upper-crust ballrooms. Dances that hardworking men and women enjoyed when spending good times amongst their friends.

Abby lost count of how many times she tossed her head back and laughed before twirling with her sisters or Laurence. She was positive she'd never had so much fun. Never felt so much joy as she did as everyone laughed, drank, danced, and simply enjoyed one another's company. Eventually, however, each sister bid her good night with an obvious look in their eyes as they reeled their husbands after them.

To that end, Laurence bid Daniel and Hugh a goodnight and pulled her after him as well. Probably a good thing because she was feeling a tad too good from the whisky. So good she wondered how well she might do with the serious conversation she and Laurence still needed to have.

"Oh dear," she exclaimed, rounding her eyes, and giggling when they arrived at the door downstairs only to find it was raining as hard as it had sounded against the panes. "How will we ever make it to our cottage in one piece, darling?"

He issued her a most rebellious grin. "Most carefully, my love, and I'm afraid it will not be in the gallant way you deserve, as I need a clear eye to the ground."

"Whatever does that mean because—"

She yelped when he hoisted her over his shoulder and dashed into the driving rain. While quite caught off guard by the position, she could not help but laugh at their circumstances. How, once again, he was saving her, only this time upside down. For whatever reason, outside of it being great fun, that only made her laugh harder.

Laugh so hard she hardly realized it when he kicked the cottage door shut behind them, and they left the dark stormy night behind. Hardly realized it until he set her down and cupped her shoulders, ensuring she was steady.

"Will you be well for a moment, love?" Just as merry as she, he gestured at the dwindling flames of a fire he must have started earlier. "I need to put wood on the fire." He shook his head and brushed back a sodden lock of hair stuck to her cheek. "Then we need to get you out of those wet clothes and dry you off."

"That sounds like a good plan indeed." She slid him a sly smile and winked. "Because I am very much having second thoughts about you, Mr. Heir-to-the-Wright fortune. Thoughts I think you will appreciate."

A small, tentative smile hovered on his mouth before he saw to the fire, and it warmed her as much as the greatest flame.

As he squatted by the hearth she took in the cottage and its many candles, then spied the bottle of champagne beside two glasses on a small wooden table. Overall, the cottage was a cozier, far more romantic oasis than she might have imagined of such a rarely used space. Luxurious blankets and pillows made the meager cot more welcoming than it might have been otherwise. If that were not enough, a rather plush comfortable-looking rug lay on the floor in front of the fire.

"You did this...you cleaned it," she murmured, eying elegant, expensive candles that had clearly come from Charles and Grace's castle. "And you..." Her smile faded, and she blinked back tears. "Yet again, you only thought of me."

Crouched in front of the fire, Laurence eyed her over his shoulder for a moment as if caught off guard by the sight of her, even though he had looked at her moments before.

"Actually, your sisters saw to everything." Seeming as drawn to her as she was to him, he closed the distance, cupped her cheek, and kept her gaze on his face. "All I did was ensure everything was worthy of you." He shook his head and looked at her with his heart in his eyes. "I tried to make you feel as comfortable as possible while on your most recent grand adventure."

"And it *has* been that" she whispered. Overwhelmed by his thoughtfulness time and time again, she dusted her fingers along his strong jaw. Wanted him so bad it hurt. "Considering I am soaking wet, I fear I have grown quite cold." She stood on her tiptoes and pulled his lips down to hers before gently kissing his mouth, then whispering in his ear, "I need to get out of this dress, love." She started pulling pins from her wet hair. "Can you help me with that?"

"I can."

Yet it seemed things might not be that easy. Clearly determined to pick up where they had left off last time they made love, he clenched his jaw, grew most serious, and backed away. "But not until we talk first, Abby." He shook his head. "I will not suffer that again."

"Suffer what?" She pulled more pins free. "Because it did not feel like either of us suffered. If anything, it felt the very opposite."

"Did it truly?" He kept shaking his head. "Because I seem to remember it in a different way."

"Do you?" She tossed away the last few pins and let her long, curly hair cascade down around her shoulders. "I distinctly recall us finding quite a bit of pleasure in one another's arms."

His breathing noticeably shifted at the sight of her hair down. To the point, she knew she was going about things the right way. The only way she could, to find the sort of pleasure she knew could exist between them.

"Talk to me, Abby." His voice was not quite right. "Please

talk to me."

"About what?" While she had been determined to put this off, the tortured look in his eyes as she pulled her dress down inch by inch made her keep going. "Reginald?"

"Yes." His gaze flickered from her bare shoulders to her face. "Very much Reginald. What it was between you."

She slid her dress lower, rebelling against her late husband as she did it. "Why?"

"I need to understand." Never taking his eyes off of her, Laurence pulled off his boots and said more than she anticipated. "And I need to understand because my mother, who was like you, a woman with a vivacious personality, ultimately betrayed my father with another man and turned from us both. My father, who had undoubtedly driven my mother away, ended up making my life hell going forward because of it. So I need to understand what Reginald did to you." Once again, his voice became a hoarse whisper. "I need to understand if you have become anything like her because of him…or might, because of me."

Honestly, it was a wonder Laurence was not a more jealous type. She wished he had told her this sooner but could not fault his hesitation as she, too, had not shared her entire past.

"No, I am not like your mother, Laurence." She blinked back more tears as she let her sodden dress flop to the floor. While some might be offended by his question, his very assumption, she saw the torture in his eyes. Emotion she knew he'd shown no other but her. "I could not be her because I know better. I was taught that men like you will only ever break my heart." She turned her back to him and pulled aside her hair, inviting him to untie her stays. "Taught that desire will soon turn to abuse because it is inevitable. That's what happened to Reginald's daughter. She died because of it."

Silence stretched before Laurence gently untied her stays and rested his temple against hers, his voice thick with emotion. "I am sorry, Abby. Sorrier than you can possibly imagine."

She gently placed her palm against the side of his head and

closed her eyes. Prayed his words were as genuine as they sounded. Sensed they were. She shuddered with a strange sort of relief when he tossed her stays aside, wrapped his arm around her from behind, and simply held her.

"I am sorry too." She could not imagine what he had suffered. "Sorry the one woman in your life who was supposed to show devotion did not. That your father—"

"Only grew more monstrous because of it." He turned her in his arms and touched her cheek lovingly, his gaze worried. "Have you not seen that same monster in me, darling? The ruthless businessman who would not take no for an answer? That would have you no matter what it took?"

"I have," she admitted, shocked to see a tiny ball of moisture at the corner of his eye. Desperate to take away his pain, she gently wiped it away. "But I have also seen a much different side. One so caring and tender it takes my breath away. Makes me want to…"

"What?" he said softly when she trailed off. "Tell me."

She shouldn't say it but could not help herself. He needed to know before he possibly broke her heart. "You make me want to love you, Laurence. Since I met you in the tavern to this very moment." She shook her head. "Love you when I had no idea I could feel such a thing. Was taught to shun it. Never trust it."

"As was I." Laurence traced her jawline, wondrous and marveling, as though touching her for the first time. "Yet I want to so much it hurts." He wrapped his large, warm hand around the back of her neck and messaged the tension from her without likely realizing he even did it. "I want to trust the way I feel about you is…"

"It's all right," she whispered, managing a small, jerky nod, understanding him so much better than she did minutes before. Understood how wary they had become by what their pasts had presented to them. She searched his eyes, never more certain or hopeful. "I think if we keep talking, keep sharing, and be honest with each other always, it will be all right."

"I have never wanted anything more," he swore, his gaze never leaving her eyes. "Never wanted anyone like I want you, Abby."

"I know." And she did, because she felt the same. To that end, she pulled his lips down to hers and kissed him so hard and so passionately that he need not doubt. Kissed him as they fell into the same frenzied passion they had lost themselves to the first time they lay together. A fevered pitch that had them yanking off the remainder of their clothes until they ended up on the carpet in front of the fire with her straddling him.

After that, everything slowed down and sped up all at once as she sank onto him, and they groaned in pleasure. Where the last time the sensations he had pulled from her had felt untouchable, never to be outdone, now everything seemed a hundred-fold more intense. A thousand-fold as they kissed, and she rode him slowly, then braced her hands on his shoulders and rode him far faster.

As she got the feel of what it was like to have a man between her legs.

The power she had over him because how else could she explain the pleasure she drew from Laurence? The way his features twisted in ecstasy when she learned to bring him just to the edge of letting go, only to slow down and draw it out.

"You are a quick learner indeed," he growled into the crook of her neck at one point. He clenched her backside and gave the side of her neck enough of a nip to arouse her all that much more. To the point she rolled her hips once, twice, only to cry out and shudder at almost the same moment he gripped her to the point of painful pleasure, yanked her down harder on his arousal, and moaned into her hair.

They stayed that way for a time, lost in the afterglow of their lovemaking before his mouth inevitably found hers again, and they started all over again until he rolled her beneath him.

"No," he murmured against her lips before he pulled away, rolled her onto her belly, and came over her until his voice was at her ear again. "This time, I am in control, love."

While she liked the sound of that, she had no idea what he meant until he gripped her hips and pulled her back until she knelt.

"Elbows on the floor, Abby," he said, his voice deep with passion now. "Palms on the carpet."

Feeling vulnerable yet excited, she did as requested, and groaned as he gripped one hip and massaged the tiny nub she had quickly learned invoked so much feeling. More so now as he built her up until he gripped both her hips and entered her from behind. Both startled and loving how good it felt, she groaned yet again and pushed back against him when he started to move.

"Laurence," she whimpered, clenching the carpet as he moved faster, and sensation became almost too much to bear. "Please…"

Driven by her request, he pressed her down until her belly hit the carpet, and he covered her from behind, body to body, their flesh hot and sweat-slickened against each other. She could feel every steamy inch of him as he didn't move more quickly but far more slowly. So slowly and so close, she clenched the carpet even harder. Sobbed with how good it felt before everything exploded, and her body was lost to such overwhelming pleasure she continued weeping.

So much pleasure that she must have drifted off because when next she awoke, she was not where she had started. Rather, she was somewhere even better.

Chapter Eighteen

I F LAURENCE HAD his way, the storm that stranded them on that little English island would have lasted forever. It would have kept him and Abby in their cozy cottage always. Would have allowed him to wake her every morning by lifting her off the carpet, laying her in bed, and continuing to make love to her until they dropped dead from exhaustion.

Unfortunately, even though they got the extra day Daniel had said they would, now it was time to go home. Under the pretense of talking things out, he and Abby had rarely emerged from their cottage, but not because they had chatted all that much. Rather they lost themselves in each other. Made love too many times to count. How could they not when she was so glorious? Like a fabled mermaid with her long, curly, wild crimson hair and a body he could not get enough of.

Not to say they did not talk.

They did, finally sharing the entirety of their pasts with one another.

"Now you understand why I grew so upset our first night together, do you not?" she asked at one point, twirling her fingers down his chest and torso toward his groin so purposely he knew lovemaking would soon again overtake conversation. "Why I was not ready to confess all?"

"I do." He'd touched her cheek affectionately and adored

looking at her. "But you did not need to, Abby. I would have understood. More than that, I would have been able to assure you…"

He tried to say it, *wanted* to say it, but still feared telling her he realized he loved her that very night. While he might not have recognized it at the time, he did now. He'd certainly hinted at it plenty since then and wanted to say it but worried it might be too much for her.

"What?" she had prompted when he'd trailed off. "What did you want to assure me of that night, Laurence?"

"How much I had come to care for you," he'd said easily enough. "Because I had. A great deal, at that."

She responded, as did he, but neither voiced the words they truly felt. Or so he hoped she felt the same but held back. Either way, they were sad to say goodbye to their little oasis when the time came.

"I will miss this place," she said as they stood at the stern of Charles's boat together and watched their lighthouse grow farther and farther away. The seas were rougher than when they had come here, but Abby seemed at ease as she kept a solid footing with the waves. She was, without doubt, comfortable on the water. A small smile curled her mouth. "I suspect I will even miss Daniel and Hugh."

"They did turn out to be quite the hosts." He grinned and considered the island. Contemplated all of it from the lighthouse to the eastern shores of England. Specifically, the cliffs on which Charles's ancestors had built his castle. Truth be told, he liked the area a great deal. "How much do you like this part of England, Abby? Would you wish to live here on and off?"

"I would," she said without hesitation. "Why do you ask?"

"Come." He took her hand and walked her to the bow so she could see what lay ahead rather than what lay behind. Having asked Charles to take them a tad south before heading north, he pointed at the tree-lined cliffs slowly emerging in the distance. "Do you see that ridge?"

Abby squinted. "I do, but barely."

"Good. Do keep an eye on it."

"All right." A small smile curled her mouth. "And why is that?"

"Because Charles and I have decided to go into business together." Laurence nodded at the area he pointed out. "And that is land I can purchase to build a second home." He shrugged. "Well, to be specific, a third home."

"I cannot tell you how happy I am to hear you will be going into business with Charles." Her smile seemed hesitant, though. "So should I assume you are building a home to be closer to your business ventures when in England?"

"You should." He looked at her most seriously. "And because I want you to be close to your sisters if you decide to marry me."

"*If* rather than *when*," Abby said softly. "Yet again, how far you have come from the arrogant all-assuming man I first met, Mr. Wright." She cocked her head. "And where will this third home of yours be?"

"Well, I should rephrase that as it will be more of a cottage than a home." He glanced back in the direction of the lighthouse, then looked at her in a way she could not mistake. "As it will be built on the isle we just left. A getaway of sorts when business becomes too stressful."

"Is that right?" she murmured, her gaze flickering back the way they had come. "And what will you do there?"

"Considering you will own half of it, you tell me." He wrapped his fingers with hers. "Because married or not, I will only ever be there if you are."

Her gaze drifted to his face and lingered momentarily before she looked at the cliffs rising in the distance. "And what will you build there, Mr. Wright?"

"Whatever your heart desires, as long as you marry no other and remain in my life."

Her brows swept up, and she dared him to be sure. "A castle as grand as Charles and Grace's?"

He hitched the corner of his mouth. "Grander if you desire." Before she could look at the cliffs again, he cupped her cheek and kept her gaze with his. "I would give you the world if I could, Abby. Every last bit of it." Though he loathed to bring it up again, as he'd only mentioned it briefly between lovemaking, he had no choice. The only way he could build and flourish was to keep working, and that meant traveling to speak with newly established business partners. "I have to see to business further south, but I will be back in time for the Christmastide Ball at MacLauchlin Castle."

He meant to say more, to ask her if she would be waiting for him and only him, yet he did not want to push. She might still owe him a dance, but that didn't truly bind her to him, not forever, and he knew it.

"The MacLauchlin's Christmastide Ball should be quite the affair," she said softly, clearly no happier than he that he would be leaving for a time.

"Knowing Blake and Maude, I expect nothing else."

"Indeed."

Outside of what rarely emerging from their cottage over the past few days implied, they had not openly shared how intimate they had grown, and he put an end to that when he reeled her into his arms and held her close. He rested her cheek against his chest, inhaled the scent of her hair, and relished the feel of her in his arms.

"I will miss you, Abby," he murmured. "Miss you more than you can possibly imagine."

"As will I, you." Clearly fine with showing just how far they had come as well, she held onto him as though she did not want to let go. "Very much so."

Because he understood she still tried to navigate her way free of the twisted knots Reginald had made her viewpoint of love into, he did not drop to a knee and propose right now. Rather, he knew the best thing at this point was for her to think about their conversations. In truth, they, *she*, had helped him understand the power his father still held over him up until he met her. Helped him understand the power Reginald still had over her even from the grave.

So, now was not the time to propose but to give her time to think about everything they had shared. Understand how much they had helped one another, because they had. *He* had, by making her see how Reginald's fears had become hers. Abby by reminding him he was not his father, and she was not his mother.

They were different people entirely.

Suffice it to say, and however difficult the parting was, he had no choice but to go his own way once they arrived back at Charles's castle. Not before he had kissed her thoroughly, let her kin make of it what they would. Kissed her so deeply her eyes remained dewy after the kiss ended and even as he and Harold climbed into their hired coach and pulled away.

"So, you are quite in love with Lady Somerset, then, sir?" Harold finally asked once he worked up the courage, or perhaps because curiosity simply got the better of him.

"Quite," he murmured and left it at that because there was nothing more to say. He might be new to this, but there was no explaining how his heart already ached with loss the moment his carriage pulled away.

Over the next month, Abby's face remained etched in his mind He was astounded at how he longed to talk with her and get her opinion on everything.

It was an unusual but not unwelcome sensation that made him realize just how much he had come to respect Abby. That he even wanted her feedback on business dealings during their time apart told him much. Every last bit of it could only be love.

While tempted to write to her, winter was upon England, and letters would travel slower, so it was best just to wait until he saw her again. Wait until he could wrap her up in his arms, kiss her silly, then talk until they inevitably made love, then talk again.

He would not risk the journey back across the Atlantic until spring, so they had time. All the time in the world, as long as she became his in the end. Or, better put, he became hers. Truth told, time seemed far too stretched as the weeks wore on. Yet what he wanted from Abby, *needed* from her, became more and more apparent, and it was not for any of the reasons he had wanted to marry into the Ton.

Rather, it was the very opposite.

So, even though he should not, he spent his spare time searching out the very best jewelers and thought long and hard about how he wanted to handle things.

"I do not understand why you are so undecided, sir," Harold said as they trudged into yet another jewelry shop. "I am sure Lady Somerset will most appreciate any ring you get her."

"It cannot be just any ring," he muttered, having learned one thing above all the past few weeks. He wanted more control of his circumstances because he felt rather adrift right now. "When we return home, I intend to learn the art of welding and jewelry making. If I can manipulate wood, I can do the same with metal."

"But, of course, sir." Yet there was a sigh and scrunch to Harold's nose as they entered the latest jewelers. Not surprising, given the building was old and stale smelling. Even so, it was where he discovered something quite unexpected. Not a proper ring by any means, or one worth all that much.

"Will you look at that," he exclaimed to Harold, smiling as he held it up. "What are the odds?"

Harold eyed it dubiously. "I cannot imagine what you mean, sir, as that is quite—"

"No, I cannot imagine you do." He clasped Harold's shoulder, quite pleased. "Yet it is almost *exactly* what I want."

Calling over the jeweler, he wondered if some adjustments might be made to it. He would pay any price. Any price at all, if Abby understood the meaning when he presented it to her. Thankfully, the adjustments could be made, and he arrived back at MacLauchlin Castle just in the nick of time.

"It seems *quite* opportunistic," Harold agreed as snow began falling heavier. "In more ways than one."

"Yes, it does," he agreed as they arrived hours before the Christmastide Ball was scheduled to begin. Torches were ablaze around MacLauchlin Castle, and festive music could already be heard inside.

"Laurence," Blake exclaimed, spying him in the courtyard upon his arrival. It seemed the laird of the castle was intent on greeting newcomers outside this evening. His friend wore a bright smile and an unexpected kilt as he skipped the formalities of a bow and embraced Laurence. "Merry Christmastide to you. I cannot tell you how glad I am to see you."

"And I, you." He smiled. "I was not sure I would make it in time, given the weather."

"Yet you have, and how welcome you are." Blake seemed a schoolboy as he grinned not just at Laurence but at everyone around him, his brogue thicker than usual. "All are so *very* welcome this fine eve."

"Indeed." He could not help but meet his friend's smile and chuckle. "And glad I am to see you so happy."

"I very much am." Blake's smile grew all that much wider. "How could I not be when we are at last expecting a wee bairn?"

"A wee what?" he asked, but it was too late. Clearly on top of the world, Blake was off to greet others, offering them the same cheery Christmastide greeting and oozing with excitement about having a wee bairn, whatever that was, on the way before he was off again.

When Laurence perked his brows at Harold, his valet grinned. "I think it is safe to say Lord and Lady MacLauchlin are expecting a child."

He smiled, then laughed and nodded. "Good news, indeed!"

Harold met his smile. "*Indeed*, sir."

What a fine blessing, as he knew Blake and Maude had long been eager for a child.

Considering he and Abby had certainly not been as prudent as they should have been when lovemaking, they had talked about it and came to only one determination. They both very much wanted children. While tempted to point out she and their child would be the ones to suffer in her upper-crust society if such happened out of wedlock, he knew better. Abby knew full well what her world looked like and seemed ready for whatever fate threw at her.

Good thing, because he intended it only ever be him and hoped, on some level, she felt the same. That she would not turn from what they had found but finally be his in all the ways that mattered.

In the way that mattered most.

So, rather than seek her out immediately, he went to his room, bathed after the long journey, and ensured Harold saw him finely presented before he went downstairs.

"This is no small thing," he muttered under his breath, more nervous than he might have imagined. He looked at his man. "You understand that, right? No small thing at all."

"I do, sir." Harold sounded quite the old fellow these days as he dished out calming advice. "And I do not doubt you will succeed as you always do at whatever you set your mind to." He straightened Laurence's cravat and looked him dead in the eyes. "This *will* happen, sir. I am certain of it." He shook his head. "Have no doubts. Not one."

"Quite right."

Bold indeed, Harold clasped his shoulders, nodded, then gave a good squeeze. "I have never once seen you back down from a battle, so do not start now, sir." He shook his head. "Not when you have come this far."

He eyed his man and nodded in return, struggling to find his confidence before he managed a solid nod. "And I shall not."

Yet as he stood in the hallway listening to the festive music below and smelled the pine and perfume drifting up from downstairs, he feared as he'd never feared before. He had traveled a ways, eager to return on this very night, but what if it was too much too soon?

What if Abby simply wanted to go back to how they had

been?

It would make sense. He might very well want to do the same in her position. Probably should until they had more time together, but he could not, no matter how long and hard he'd thought about it. He had never felt this way about a woman, and while he would not make her his via some contract if she denied him, he would give Abby his very best shot.

That, ironically, meant fulfilling their contract here.

Now.

Tonight.

So when he emerged into the great hall via a back way and spied her coming down the stairs, he knew there was no backing out of this, nor would he ever want to. She was stunning in a bluish-green shimmering dress that matched her eyes. Even though her hair was swept back, he only saw it down around her shoulders in the heat of passion. The flush in her cheeks as she moaned and wrapped her legs around him as he thrust deep.

Then he saw her sound asleep the next morning, her red hair vibrant in the dim daylight, as though it wanted to stand out no matter what. As if it was determined to be as vivacious and beautiful as her. He had not been able to get enough of its silky texture. The way it felt as he dug his hands into it and buried himself in her body until she cried out in pleasure.

Yet always, after all the intense passion, he would kiss her. Hold her. Fold her up in his arms until it seemed they were one. Mingled limbs. Loving caresses. Incredible sensual pleasure but at the same time friendship. Touching moments when they absently stroked and touched one another and talked. Fell in love, or so he hoped.

And it all led to this moment.

Abby walking down the stairs.

This was his moment. Her moment. *Their* moment.

So he did not hesitate to cut through the crowd with one question and one question only. Now only one thing remained. How would she answer him?

Chapter Nineteen

"**A**RE YOU ALL right, dear sister?" Abby asked Maude, rubbing her back as she lingered over the chamber pot. She frowned at Prudence and Grace, who cared for her. One pressed a cool cloth to Maude's forehead and the other to her neck to soothe her. "It is foolish holding such a ball tonight. This castle's lady is with child, so it should be canceled."

"That is the most ridiculous thing I have ever heard." Maude shoved away the smelling salts Prudence tried to wave under her nose. "It is Christmastide and a most special time of the year here at MacLauchlin Castle." She gestured at the icy window, and her eyes lit with joy even if dimmed by nausea. "Plus, it is snowing. How *utterly* perfect!"

"Then what would you have us do?" Grace said, clearly not pleased.

"I would have you go enjoy the ball," Maude made clear. "Entertain my guests and look after Blake if you would." A small smile hovered on her mouth. "I fear he is a bit childlike in his upcoming fatherly glee and does need some reining in." She looked from sister to sister and chuckled. "So I task you with that and expect, as your Christmastide gift to me, that you shall see him looked after and everyone well-entertained this holiday."

Before any could deny her, Maude shot them her infamous *Big Sister Has Final Say* look and laid back on the settee. "I am going to rest for a bit, then try my best to join you all soon."

"Rest well, then, sweet sister." Grace sighed and kissed Maude's cheek before departing. "We will see to your requests, including our dear brother-by-marriage."

"Indeed." Prudence kissed her other cheek and left.

"Abby," Maude murmured before Abby did the same.

"Yes, darling." She took her sister's hand. "Do you wish me to stay because I will? We could talk or play word games as we did in our youth or—"

"Good God, no." Maude managed a weak smile. "You have always been a sore loser when I inevitably outdo you with words, so best we not."

"I am *not* a sore loser," she exclaimed, quite taken aback.

"Oh, dear me, but you are." Maude squeezed her hand and smirked. "Fortunately, that is part of your adventuresome spirit and the need to conquer all that was not fully taken from you by Reginald, and I could not be happier for it."

"I am sure I do not know what you mean."

"Do you not?" Maude wrapped her fingers with Abby's and looked at her with such love, she was eternally grateful she had been blessed with sisters.

"You have been quite close-lipped about your time with Mr. Wright at the lighthouse cottage, but we all see it. Saw the way he kissed you before departing a month ago." Maude smiled. "And we are all so very happy you found love at last. I wanted you to know that before you went downstairs."

She made to reply, but Maude's eyes slid shut.

Indeed, she *had* found love in a very short time, and how incredibly intense it was. She never stopped thinking about Laurence. Not for a second. Where was he now? Had his business deals worked out? Was he on his way back to her? She had no idea as he had not written. Not a word. And though she'd assured her sisters it was fine, that he was busy, it had stung.

She longed for him by day and even more by night.

Yet, no word. Silence. So perhaps he had returned to America? Maybe it was just as Reginald had warned, and he would only break her heart? She sighed and tried not to dwell on it. If Laurence had been disingenuous in the time they spent together, then she would die an old spinster because he would be the epitome of what Reginald had said men were really capable of.

"You look so very beautiful, sister," she swore Maude whispered, but when she turned back to look at her from the door, her sister appeared sound asleep, so she made her way down to the festivities.

The castle had been decked out beautifully with holly, ribbons, ivy, and fir branches. Round kissing boughs decorated with fruit and candles hung here and there, temping yuletide romance. The air smelled of evergreen and spices, and a lovely rendition of *Here We Come a-Wassailing* drifted from the ballroom.

It was all splendid and perfect, but despite the sea of welcoming faces when she got downstairs, she wanted to be close if Maude needed her. Yes, her sister could ring for a maid, but why not have a sibling close instead? She deserved that for all the kindness she had shown others. For how good of a big sister she had been to Abby, Grace, and Prudence.

So she returned to the sizeable sitting room beside Maude's chamber and sat near the crackling fire. Then, she fingered the pendant Laurence had made for her that hung religiously around her neck, rested her head back, and closed her eyes.

The wind howled outside, and sleet mixed with snow, tapping against the windows, bringing her back to the stormy night in their cottage. Rain had pelted the window as she and Laurence made love, then held each other afterward. It felt like he was right there with her again for a moment. Adoring her as only he could.

"Abby," he whispered.

When she heard his voice, her eyes shot open. Was that truly him crouching in front of her, or was she dreaming? Because he looked at her with as much love as he had when last they parted.

"Laurence," she managed hoarsely, touching his cheek, wanting to make sure he was real. "Is that you? Are you really here?"

"It is, and I am." He smiled and cupped her cheek in return as though he had longed to do so since last they met. "Why do you seem so surprised, my love? Surely you knew I would come back?"

"Of course." She bit her lower lip and fought tears. "Though I confess I might have let Reginald's words influence my thoughts again."

"Well, whatever they might have been, he was wrong." He pulled her up into his arms and showed her just how wrong her late husband had been with a deep, passionate kiss. One that might not have ended had Maude not cracked the door open and peeked out.

"I thought I heard someone out here." Her eyes lit with happiness, and she smiled warmly at Laurence. "Welcome back, Laurence. Wishing you a very Merry Christmastide."

"Wishing the same to you, my lady." He pulled away from Abby reluctantly and returned Maude's smile. "I hear you and Lord MacLauchlin are expecting a child. I wish you nothing but joy ahead."

"May God keep him or her safe." Seeming a tad better, Maude sighed with pleasure and glanced from Abby to Laurence. "Now that you have returned as I very much knew you would, I was wondering if I might ask a favor of you, Laurence? Perhaps consider it a gift at the holidays?"

"Of course." His smile only grew. "How might I assist you?"

"It is actually a request that you assist Abby and see through the rest of your contract so my lovely sister can finally find peace."

"Goodness, sister," Abby exclaimed. "Why are you worried about—"

"Indeed, I will," Laurence said, cutting her off. "As that was my very intention when I arrived here tonight." He considered the sizeable room, then looked at Maude. "Here, then, or downstairs?"

"Oh, here would be positively lovely." Maude clasped her hands in delight. "It truly would make me feel part of the festivities."

Abby shook her head. "Surely not when you hardly feel well."

Maude kept smiling. "I am plenty well enough to watch you dance."

"So it seems, my dear, and it does my heart good," Blake said, having appeared at the door at some point. "And I could not agree more." He urged Maude to sit beside him on a settee, held her hand, and gestured from Laurence and Abby to the spacious area in front of the fire. "To that end, I think you two should finally put your contract behind you." He tilted his ear to the music drifting up. "And what perfect timing, as it sounds like a waltz has just begun."

"That it has." Looking quite dapper indeed, Laurence bowed at the waist, held out his gloved hand to Abby, and looked at her in a way that made her heart flutter. "If you would, Lady Somerset?"

Should she? *Dare* she?

Yes, at long last, very much *yes*.

The moment she slipped her hand into his, Laurence pulled her into his arms and twirled her away from Maude and Blake as the waltz below swung into motion. There might be less space than downstairs, but it mattered little. Laurence was as good at this as he was at everything else, swirling her so smoothly he took her breath away.

Waltzing with him was entirely different than it had been with Reginald. Where her late husband had been stiff and hardly looked at her, Laurence gazed at her with adoration. He made her feel like she was being swept off her feet. As always, everything faded away but him, and what they felt and the magic that seemed to ignite between them. A magic that only intensified when the waltz eventually came to an end, and he fell to a knee, then presented a ring to her.

A ring that brought fresh tears to her eyes.

"Oh, Laurence," she whispered, staring at the tiny outline of a building designed into the heart of the band that looked very much like a tavern. Moreover, she stared at the gemstones nestled within it. One the color of her eyes and one the shade of his, no doubt reflecting the moment they had first locked gazes.

"Marry me, Abby," Laurence asked, or perhaps a tad demanded, as he looked at her with unabashed love. "Marry me, because I love you dearly. Because I want to share the rest of my life and endless adventures with you."

"Was that a question—" she smiled, and her throat thickened with emotion—"or yet another demand?"

"Perhaps a bit of both." Laurence grinned and gazed at her with so much adoration it made her heart hurt. "All I know is I don't want to travel one town over, let alone across the world, ever again without you by my side."

"Nor should you," Maude echoed happily from the background.

"Much agreed," Blake said, backing her up.

Both went on to say why, but it was too late. Abby had already said, "Yes," and then adored the feel of Laurence sliding the ring on her finger. Better still, she cherished the feelings created when he stood, pulled her into his arms, and kissed her deeply.

In fact, she cherished every hour of every day she spent with him after that in a lifetime full of untouchable love and boundless adventures. As promised, he built her a castle on the cliffs just south of Grace and Charles's castle and a cottage of their own on the lighthouse island. She sailed across the Atlantic and made lots of new friends in Boston, then sailed on to visit many new and interesting destinations.

Sometimes on his ship and other times on hers.

Their greatest adventure, however, was the birth of their son the following year, who came shortly after Maude and Blake's little girl. If that were not enough, she and Laurence were blessed with another son and a daughter, each every bit as adventuresome as their parents. Blessings that made her grateful she had bumped into an American in a tavern and finally fallen in love.

More so and above all, that in the end, she'd had second thoughts about the heir.

THE END

About the Author

Sky Purington is the bestselling author of over fifty novels and novellas. A New Englander born and bred who recently moved to Virginia, Purington married her hero, has an amazing son who inspires her daily and two ultra-lovable husky shepherd mixes. Passionate for variety, Sky's vivid imagination spans several romance genres, including historical, time travel, paranormal, and fantasy. Expect steamy stories teeming with protective alpha heroes and strong-minded heroines.

Purington loves to hear from readers and can be contacted at Sky@SkyPurington.com. Interested in keeping up with Sky's latest news and releases? Either visit Sky's website, www.SkyPurington.com, join her quarterly newsletter, or sign up for personalized text message alerts. Simply text 'skypurington' (no quotes, one word, all lowercase) to 74121 or visit Sky's Sign-up Page. Texts will ONLY be sent when there is a new book release. Readers can easily opt out at any time.

Love social networking? Find Sky on Facebook, Instagram, Twitter, and Goodreads.

Want a few more options? "Follow" Sky Purington on Amazon to receive New Release Kindle Updates and "Follow" Sky on BookBub to be notified of amazing upcoming deals.

www.ingramcontent.com/pod-product-compliance
Lightning Source LLC
Chambersburg PA
CBHW060409310726
48976CB00003B/990